My Body

STUDENT'S BOOK

TERM 1 GRADE 2

Margaret Bailey • June Blythe-Livingston
Maureen Byfield • Beverley Dinnall • Winnifred Whittaker

MACMILLAN
CARIBBEAN

Macmillan Education
Between Towns Road, Oxford OX4 3PP
A division of Macmillan Publishers Limited
Companies and representatives throughout the world

www.macmillan-caribbean.com

ISBN 978-1-4050-0738-2

Text © Margaret Bailey, June Blythe-Livingston, Maureen Byfield,
Beverly Dinnall, Derek McMonagle, Winnifred Whittaker and Pauline Anning 2006
Design and illustration © Macmillan Publishers Limited 2006

Editorial Consultants: Derek McMonagle and Pauline Anning

First published 2006

All rights reserved; no part of this publication may be
reproduced, stored in a retrieval system, transmitted in any
form or by any means, electronic, mechanical, photocopying,
recording, or otherwise, without the prior written permission
of the publishers.

Typeset by Kamae Design
Illustrated by Val Biro, Gillian Chapman/Linden Artists,
Simon Rumble; Jim Eldridge/Beehive Illustration/
Errol Stennett, Tek-Art
Cover design by Jason Billin
Cover photograph by Franz Marzouca

Printed and bound in Malaysia

2016 2015 2014 2013 2012 2011
10 9 8 7 6 5

Contents

Term 1

1	What do I need to know about my brain, heart and skeleton?	6
2	How do these parts work together?	46
3	How do we differ in size?	65
4	How do I keep my body healthy?	91
5	What do I do to be safe (at home, at school, on the road)?	128
6	How do others take care of me?	167

For the teacher

Macmillan Primary Integrated Curriculum is the first in a comprehensive series of books covering the requirements of the entire Jamaica primary curriculum. The books have been written by an experienced team of writers who have both an in-depth knowledge of primary education in Jamaica and the ability to present the content in a way which will appeal to young students.

The topics of this book follow the same sequence as in the curriculum document. However, in recognising that, there is a good deal of material to be covered in the time available, and some procedures and activities have been grouped together where the authors thought appropriate, but without losing the essential detail of the curriculum.

The focus questions from the curriculum have been adopted as chapter headings so that the teacher can very easily relate the course content to that of the curriculum. Each topic within a chapter has a component in the Student's Book, the Workbook and the Teacher's Guide.

All written exercises are in the Workbook so the Student's Book is not written on at all and only the Workbook needs to be replaced year on year.

In the Teacher's Guide, comprehensive notes amounting to a suggested lesson plan are given, together with stated aims and objectives, key words, any materials needed for the lesson and details of assessment and evaluation.

In order to provide a truly integrated course, suitable exercises for use in Mathematics and Language Arts Windows have been included in many topics.

The content provides a variety of different sorts of activities which will allow all students to enjoy positive achievement by demonstrating those skills in which they are competent, be they writing, working with materials or performing in some way.

Structure of the series

In the first three years the content is totally integrated with a separate Student's Book and Workbook for each term and a Teacher's Book for each year containing extensive teaching notes for each chapter.

	Student's Books	Workbooks	Teacher's Books
Year 1	Term 1 All About Me Term 2 My Family Term 3 My School	Term 1 All About Me Term 2 My Family Term 3 My School	Teacher's Book 1
Year 2	Term 1 My Body Term 2 Living Together Term 3 My Community	Term 1 My Body Term 2 Living Together Term 3 My Community	Teacher's Book 2
Year 3	Term 1 How Does My Body Work? Term 2 Culture Term 3 My Environment	Term 1 How Does My Body Work? Term 2 Culture Term 3 My Environment	Teacher's Book 3

For Grades 4-6 there are separate books for the different disciplines. The following Macmillan courses have been developed for primary students and teachers in the Caribbean:

- Primary English - *Language Tree* Grades 4-6
- Primary Mathematics - *Bright Sparks* Grades 4-6
- Primary Science - *Bright Ideas* Grades 4-6
- *Primary Social Studies for Jamaica* Grades 4-6 (forthcoming).

For all these courses, each Student's Book has an accompanying Workbook and Teacher's Book.

There is also a wide range of teacher's resources (lesson plans and worksheets) for *Language Tree, Bright Sparks, Bright Ideas* and *Social Studies* that are freely downloadable from the Teacher Resources section of the Macmillan Caribbean website: www.macmillan-caribbean.com .

What do I need to know about my brain, heart and skeleton?

1.1 Inside my body

My skeleton

Think of the reason you are able to stand upright.

Your body has something to keep it upright. It is your *skeleton*.
All the bones in the body make up the skeleton.
It holds your flesh and protects your *internal organs*.
It gives your body shape.

Your skeleton makes it possible for you to sit, stand, walk, run and have balance.

An adult has fewer bones than a baby.
This is because when a baby is born some of the bones are not fused together.
As the baby gets older, bones fuse or join together.

If your heart, lung or brain is not healthy, you must see a doctor. You may even need to see a special doctor.

Words to know

cardiologist   a doctor who takes care of the heart
neurosurgeon   a doctor who takes care of the brain

Look again at the picture of the skeleton.
You will see that all the bones are not the same size or shape.
Some are very tiny, others are straight, curved or broad.
The smallest bone in your body is found in your ear. The biggest bone is found in the thigh.
Where two bones meet is called a *joint*.

Making bones strong

Think of a baby you know.
Why can't this baby stand or sit upright?
If you said the bones are not yet firm enough, you are correct.

As your bones grow, you get taller.

You need to eat the right food to help your bones grow strong.

Foods such as milk and cheese make your bones strong.

These foods have a mineral called *calcium*.

This is the mineral that makes bones grow strong.

Page 9

Writing a friendly letter

Briana was not at school when Miss James taught the children about the skeleton.

Her best friend, Brandon, wrote a letter to her telling her about the lesson. Read Brandon's letter.

> Lime Hall
> Guys Hill P.O.
> St Catherine
> March 13, 2006
>
> Dear Briana,
> Today Miss James taught us about the skeleton. Did you know that the skeleton gives our body its shape and helps us to stay upright?
> I will tell you more about it when I see you next week.
>
> Your friend,
> Brandon

Your body has many parts. A letter has many parts. Here are the main parts of a letter:

The address: Lime Hall
Guys Hill P.O.
St Catherine

The date: March 13, 2006

The greeting: Dear Briana,

The body: What you say in the letter

The closing: Your friend,
Brandon

Discuss what else you could tell Briana about the skeleton.

What do I need to know about my brain?

Riddle: Riddle me dis, riddle me dat,
Guess mi dis riddle and perhaps not.

Which helmet cannot be taken off?

The skull is like a crash helmet that protects your brain.

If your brain is damaged, you might not be able to move about.

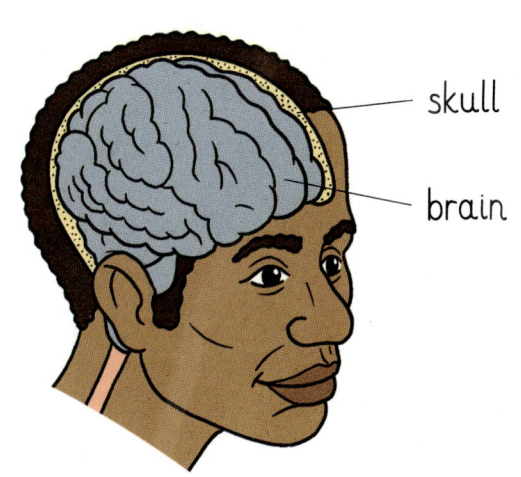

Page 13

Protecting your skull

Protect your skull by wearing your helmet when you need to. For example, wear it when riding your bicycle or skate boarding.

Interesting facts about my brain:
- My brain is always working, even when I am asleep.
- My brain controls my heartbeat, breathing and other body functions.
- My brain never lies down on the job. I always use my brain to think good thoughts and do my lessons well.

What do I need to know about my heart?

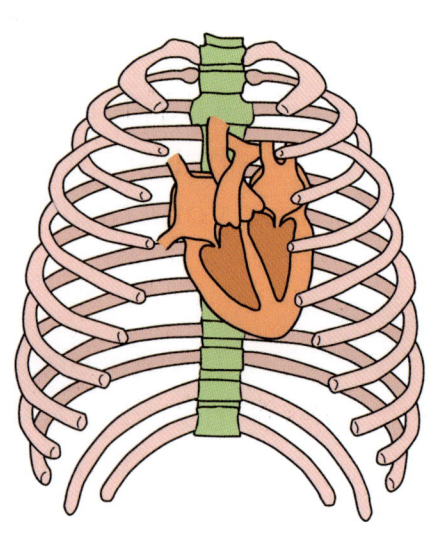

Look at the picture and talk about it.

Count the bones of the rib cage.

How many organs can you see in the rib cage?

The heart is an organ.

It is protected by the bones of the rib cage.

Page 14

Brilliant Brenda

This is Brilliant Brenda. She loves words, especially those starting with 'br'.

Read the words that Brenda is reading.
She wrote some of her favourite words in her book.
She wrote them under their pictures. Here they are:

Call each word aloud. Where do you hear the 'br' sound?
Make sentences with the words and read them to the class.

Numbers and the body

Use your body to count.

Read this passage with the person next to you.

I have one (1) head.
I have two (2) ears.
I can show three (3) fingers on my hand.
When I crawl on my hands and feet I can say I am on all fours (4).
Here is a set of five (5) fingers on one hand.
Five (5) fingers plus one finger makes six (6) fingers.
Five (5) toes plus two (2) toes makes seven (7) toes.
Five (5) fingers plus three (3) fingers makes eight (8) fingers.
Five (5) toes plus four (4) toes makes nine (9) toes.
Two sets of five (5) fingers make one (1) set of ten (10) fingers.

1.3 A dictionary of body parts

My body dictionary

A dictionary is a book of words and their meanings.

The words are arranged in ABC or alphabetical order.

A dictionary gives the meaning of words. It can help us to spell words correctly. Some dictionaries have pictures to help us understand the meaning of the words.

Everyone should have a dictionary handy.

Let us read the meanings of these words.

Word	Meaning
brain	The organ that controls thinking and movement.
chest	The upper front part of the body.
flesh	The soft substance that covers the bones and lies under the skin.
heart	The organ in the body that pumps blood to the other parts.
joint	Place in the body where two bones meet.
lungs	The pair of organs in the chest that allows us to breathe.
skeleton	All the bones in the body that give it shape.
skin	The outer covering of the body.
skull	The bones of the head that protect the brain.
torso	The human body (this does not include the head or arms and legs).

Tens and ones

Sets that have ten (10) or more members can be divided into groups of tens and ones.

Remember that the body has many bones.
They can be divided into groups of tens and ones.
Let us count the bones in the fingers and write the numerals in tens and ones.

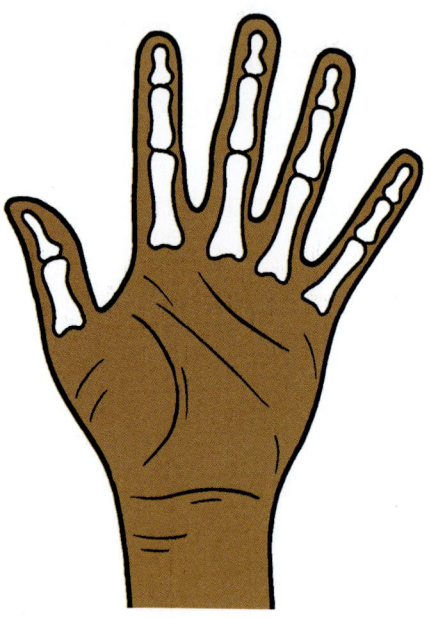

There are 14 bones in the fingers. We could share them into 1 group of ten and 4 ones.

We can also write it like this:

Tens   Ones
1   4

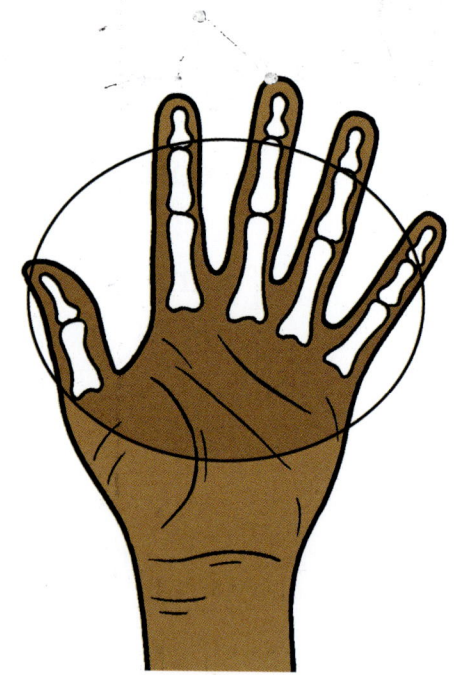

Page 20

More about tens and ones

Let us look at some other examples of tens and ones.

10 birds
ten birds
How many groups of 10 and how many ones?

15 sweets
fifteen sweets
How many groups of 10 and how many ones?

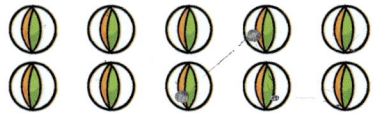

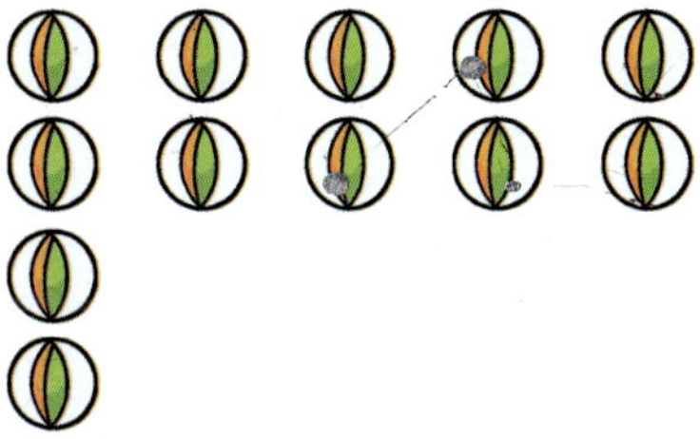

12 marbles
twelve marbles
How many groups of 10 and how many ones?

23 eggs
twenty three eggs
How many groups of 10 and how many ones?

1.4 Body map

Look at the diagram of the human skeleton.

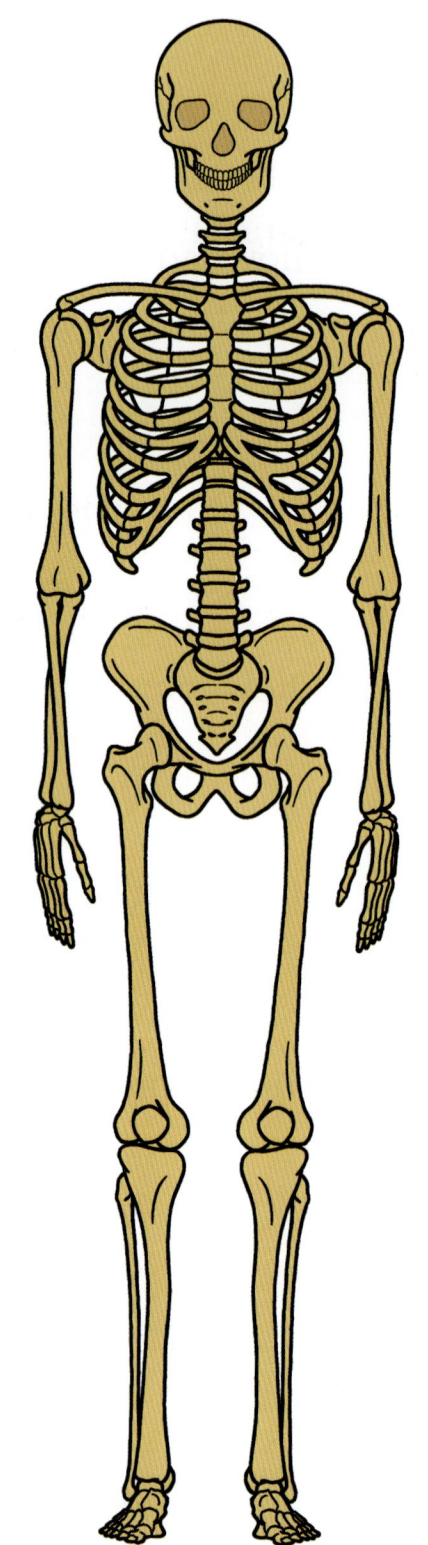

This diagram is like a map.

A map is a drawing or a picture that shows where things or places are located.

Sing the song 'Dry Bones' and do the actions.

Sing the song again.

This time, use the diagram to locate the bones that are mentioned in the song.

1.5 Heartbeat

When the heart contracts and relaxes, this is known as a heartbeat.
Remember: a heartbeat happens when your heart squeezes together then relaxes.

Check your heartbeat.

Walk slowly to the playfield.
Place your hand on your chest where your heart is. Can you feel your heart beating? How is it beating?

Now run back to the classroom.
Check your heartbeat again. How is it beating this time?

It is beating much faster. This is because when you move very fast, the heart works harder to pump blood around the body more quickly.

The faster you move the faster your heart works.

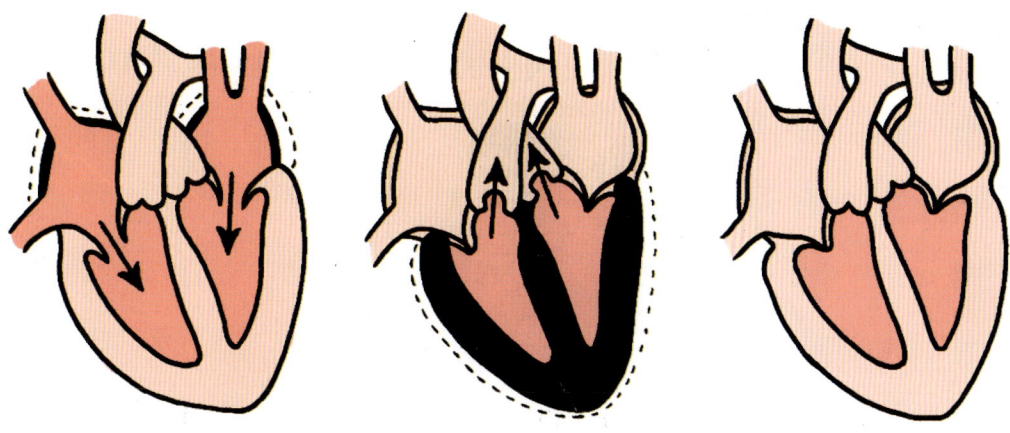

More about your heartbeat

Your heart is about the size of your fist.
Close your hand into a loose fist.
Now squeeze hard. Relax.
Squeeze hard, relax.

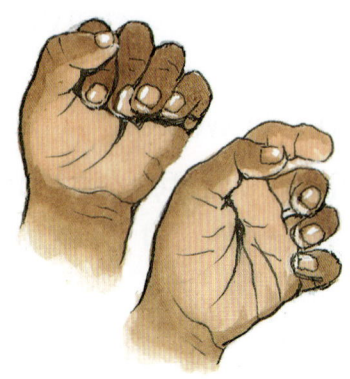

This exercise helps to explain
the way your heart works.
First it squeezes together or
contracts, and then it loosens
or relaxes.
This happens about 90 times in
one minute when you are relaxed.

It works more rapidly when you are running or jumping.

Compound words

The word heartbeat can be divided into two small words: **heart** and **beat**.

heart   is the organ that pumps blood all over the body.
beat   means rhythmic movement or sound.

Here are some other compound words.
Look at the pictures and say the compound words.

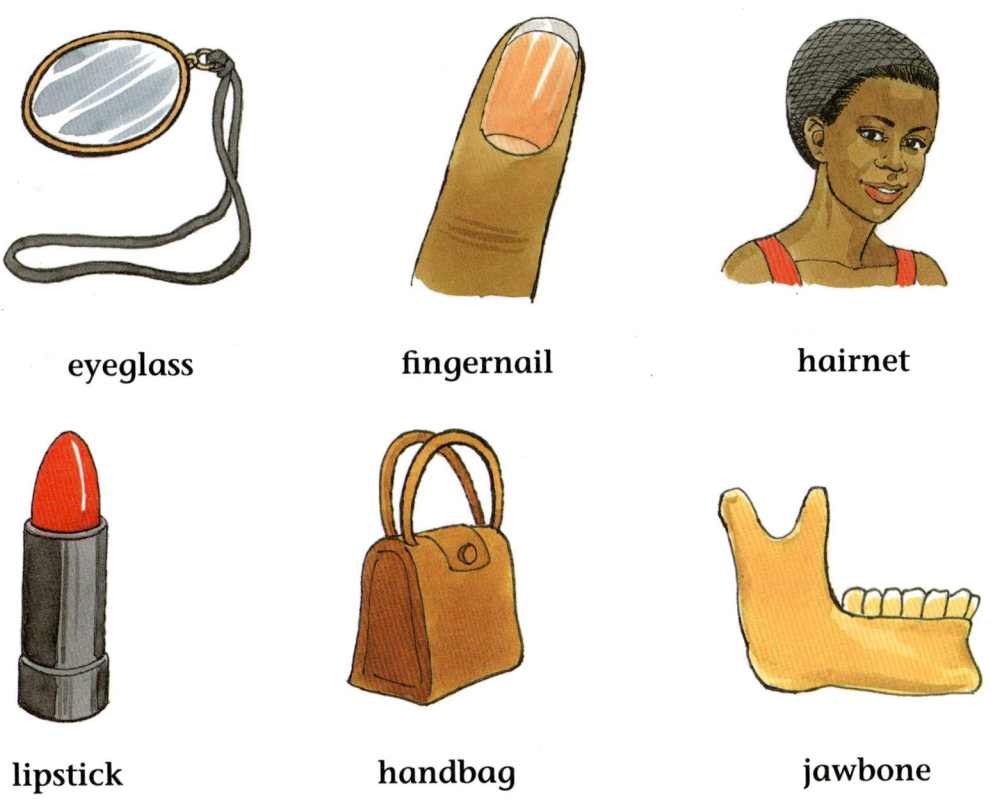

eyeglass   fingernail   hairnet

lipstick   handbag   jawbone

Now say the two small words that make up each compound word.
Talk about the meaning of each small word.
Check your dictionary to see how well you are doing.

More about compound words

Point out any of the things below that might be in your classroom.

flowerpot   chalkboard   bookcase

doorknob   schoolbag   cupboard

Jesus helped Jairus's daughter

Read this story.

Story: **The Girl who got Back her Heartbeat**

Long ago while Jesus lived on earth, a man named Jairus had a daughter.
She was about twelve years old.
The little girl got sick and although her family took good care of her, she died.
She had no heartbeat. Her family was very sad.

They cried a lot.
They invited Jesus to the home.
He told the people that the girl was not dead, she was only sleeping.
This made the people laugh at him.

Jesus went inside the house and held the girl's hand.
Immediately her heart started to beat again and she came back to life.

Everyone was happy.

Measurement

We use a clock to measure time.
Clocks measure time in seconds, minutes and hours.
Let us look at this clock face.

The long hand is the minute hand.
The short hand is the hour hand.

The minute hand is longer than the hour hand.

This hour hand is pointing to the number 8.
This minute hand is pointing to the number 12
This clock is telling us that it is 8 o'clock.

Talk about these clocks with your teacher.

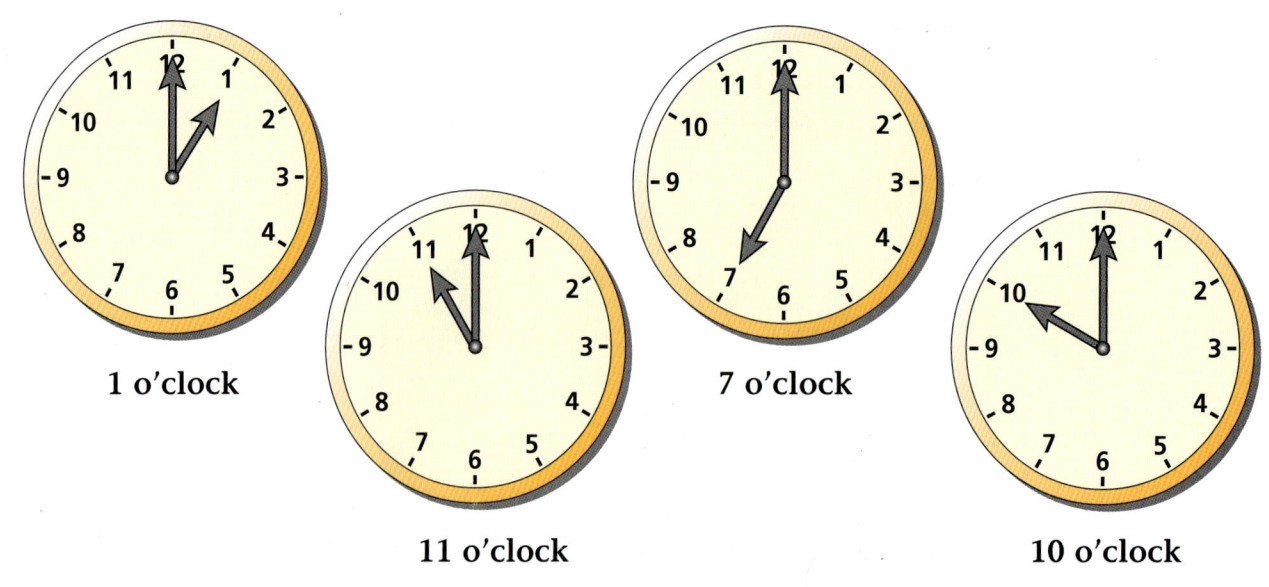

1 o'clock

11 o'clock

7 o'clock

10 o'clock

Page 30

1.6 Measuring my heartbeat

Clocks measure time in seconds, minutes and hours. Heartbeat is measured by counting the number of beats in one minute.

A doctor uses a special instrument to listen to the heartbeat.
It is called a *stethoscope*.

Take turns listening to your classmate's heartbeat.
Count the number of beats you hear in one minute.

Interesting facts about your heartbeat:
- The human adult heart beats about 90 times in one minute when the person is resting.
- When someone exercises their heart beats faster.
- Animals' hearts beat at different rates.
- The bigger the animal the slower its heart beats.

A hummingbird's heart beats between 400 and 500 times each minute.

A human child's heart beats between 80 and 100 times each minute. As you grow older your heart beats more slowly.

An elephant's heart beats between 20 and 30 times each minute.

Words that sound the same but have different meanings

Do you know the difference between '**beat**' and '**beet**'?
Did you say that they sound the same but have different meanings?
Well, you are correct!

There are many words that have the same sound and name but different meanings and spellings.

Look at the pictures and say the words.

hair/hare   stake/steak   pear/pair   flower/flour

These pictures stand for words that sound the same but have different meanings.

Talk about each pair of words and make up a sentence that has each word in it.

> Tell other words that sound the same but have different meanings.

1.7 Body songs

Sing about the body

There are many songs that tell about parts of the body. Let us sing some of these songs about the body.

Song: **Clap Your Hands**

> Clap your tiny hands
> Clap your tiny hands
> Clap your tiny hands for joy
> Jesus loves to hear, little children sing
> Clap your tiny hands for joy.

Song: **Be Careful Little Hands**

Oh be careful little hands what you do
Oh be careful little hands what you do
Because there is a Father up above
Looking down with tender love
So be careful little hands what you do.

Oh be careful little ears what you hear
Oh be careful little ears what you hear
Because there is a Father up above
Looking down with tender love
So be careful little ears what you hear.

Be careful little eyes what you see
Be careful little eyes what you see
Because there is a Father up above
Looking down with tender love
So be careful little eyes what you see.

Be careful little feet where you go
Be careful little feet where you go
Because there is a Father up above
Looking down with tender love
So be careful little feet where you go.

Song: **Joy Joy**

I have a joy, joy, joy down in my heart
Down in my heart, down in my heart
And it's down in my heart to stay.
And I'm so happy, so very happy,
I've got the love of Jesus in my heart.

I've got the John 3:16 down in my heart. Where?
Up in my head. Where? All over me
And it's down in my heart to stay
And I'm so happy. So very happy,
I've got the love of Jesus in my heart.

Song: **Ten Tiny Fingers**

I have ten tiny fingers
I have ten tiny toes
I have two eyes
I have two ears
I have a little nose
My hands are ever ready to clap one, two, three, four
My feet are ever ready to stomp upon the floor.

1.9 Taking pictures of the inside of my body

Looking back

S   is for my skull which protects my brain.
K   is for my knee, a hinge joint.
E   is for elbow, another hinge joint.
L   is for the legs; I can hop about on one.
E   eyes, ears and elbow all start with this letter.
T   starts tongue, touch and teeth.
O   is for organs; my body has many.
N   is for neck which bears my head.

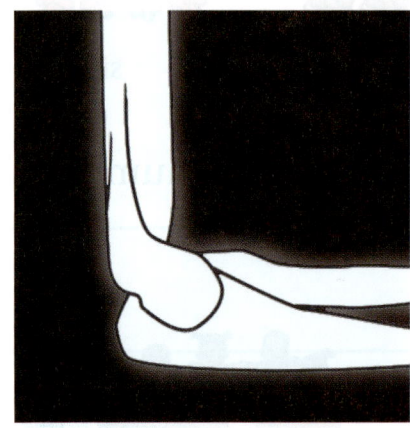 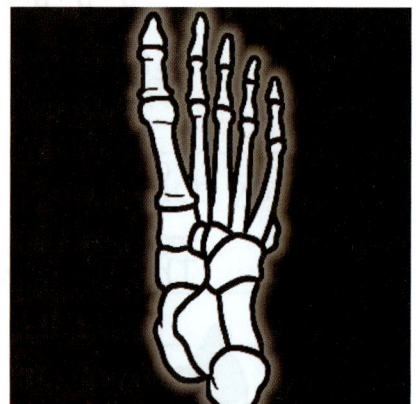

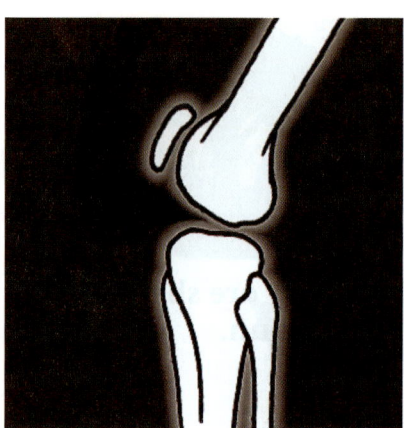

Sometimes when the doctor examines us he cannot tell what is wrong so he sends us to get an *X-ray* done.

An X-ray is a picture of the inside of the body. These pictures are taken by specially trained people called *X-ray technicians*.

1.10 Skeletons of other animals

Remember our bones make up our skeleton.
Your skeleton is *inside* your body, so it is also called an *endoskeleton*.
Animals like fish, birds and cows have an endoskeleton.
Bones make up their skeleton and give their bodies shape.
Like us, their skeletons help them to move about.

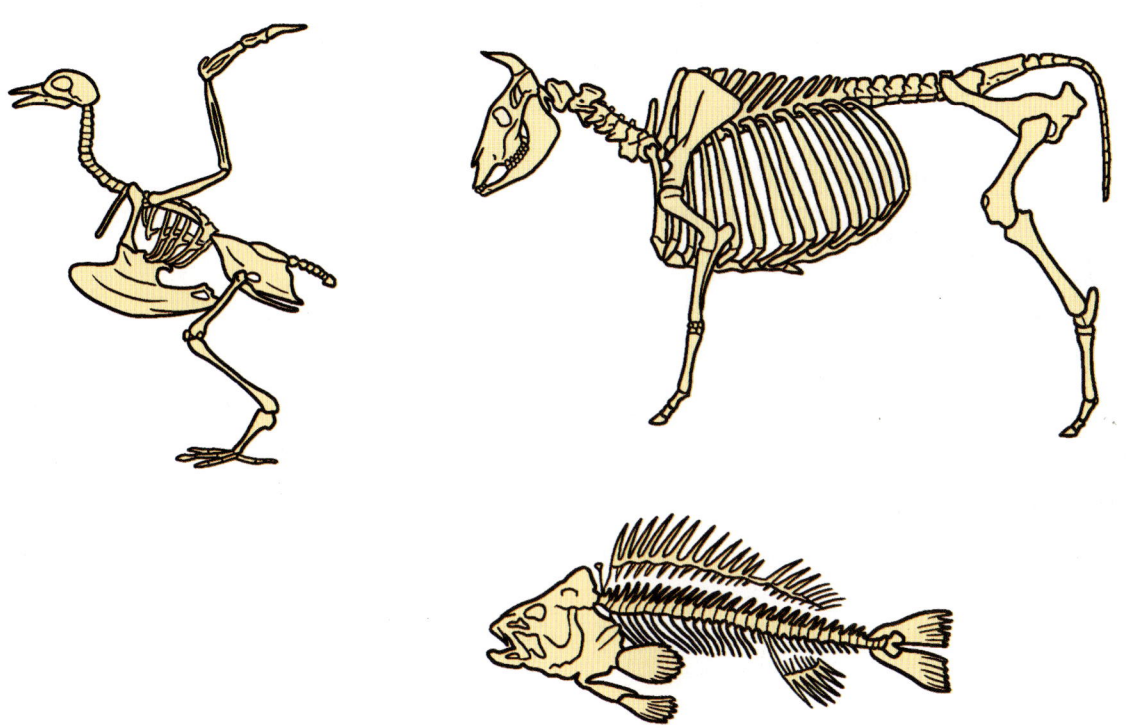

Interesting facts about bones:
- Bones in the skeleton are shaped and connected in different ways.
- Bones can be long or short, round or flat.
- A bird has very light hollow bones so that it can fly more easily.
- A cow has very strong bones to carry its heavy weight.
- A fish has a very flexible backbone to help it swim.

More about skeletons

Look at the skeletons of these animals.

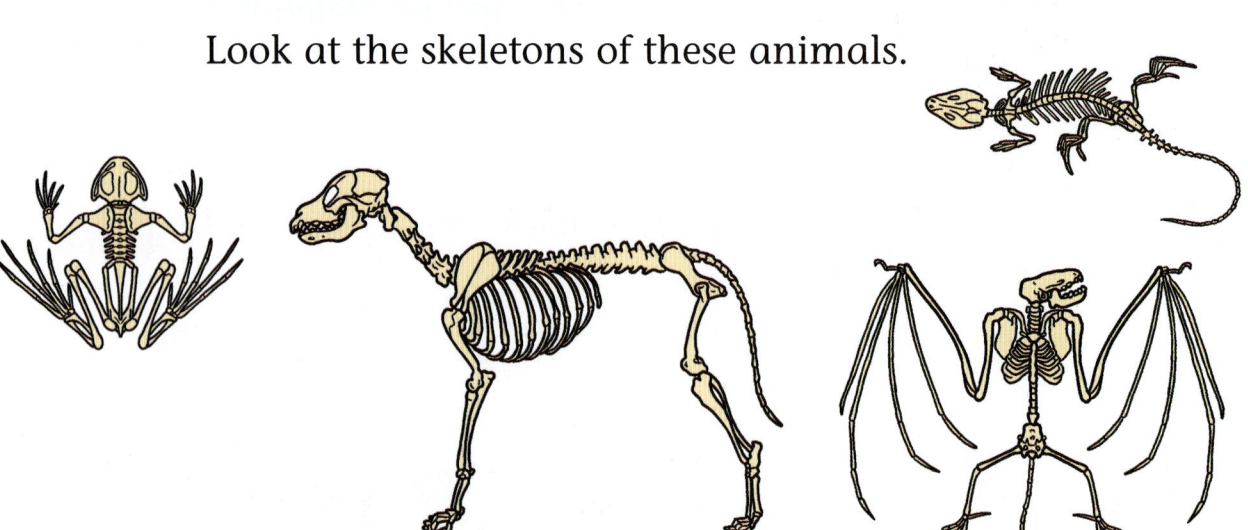

Do they have the shape of the animals they represent? Discuss this with your teacher.

Numbers to one hundred

1	2	3	4	5	6	7	8	9	10
11	12	13	14	15	16	17	18	19	20
21	22	23	24	25	26	27	28	29	30
31	32	33	34	35	36	37	38	39	40
41	42	43	44	45	46	47	48	49	50
51	52	53	54	55	56	57	58	59	60
61	62	63	64	65	66	67	68	69	70
71	72	73	74	75	76	77	78	79	80
81	82	83	84	85	86	87	88	89	90
91	92	93	94	95	96	97	98	99	100

Notice that on this grid the numbers are placed in *serial order.*

Serial order means that in each line all the numbers end with the same numeral.

If we count numbers in 10s it would go like this.
Let us touch each number as we call it.

10   20   30   40   50   60   70   80   90   100

Count in 5s with a classmate.

1.11 Poems about bones

Poem: **No Bones!**

A life with no bones!
I cannot understand
How would I stand?
And how would I stretch or bend?

No bones!
What would my shape be?
And where would my brain be?
I just don't know.

Thank God for strong healthy bones
I can lift heavy stones
Hold my head up high
And walk every day with pride.

Beverley Dinnall

Poem: **How Many Bones**

Have you ever stopped to think
How many bones there are?
In our bodies big or small
Or those bodies short or tall.

Babies have more bones you see,
Than adults like our moms and dads,
Adults are older with stronger bones
To keep them upright, fit and strong.

Winnifred Whittaker

1.12 Stories about body parts

The story of the lungs

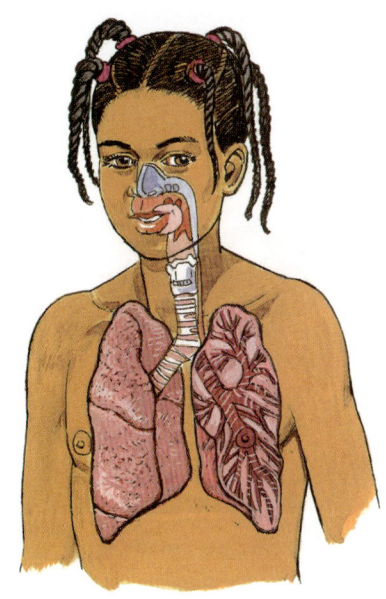

Read about your lungs.

We are your lungs and we help you to breathe.
We are a pinkish-grey colour.
Did you know that we are twin organs found in your chest, under your ribs?
The ribs help to keep us safe.
A number of diseases such as asthma and bronchitis can affect us.
These can be treated with medicines.
Sometimes the medicine is in an inhaler.

1.13 The brain as a machine

The brain is like a machine.
It has many different parts like a machine.

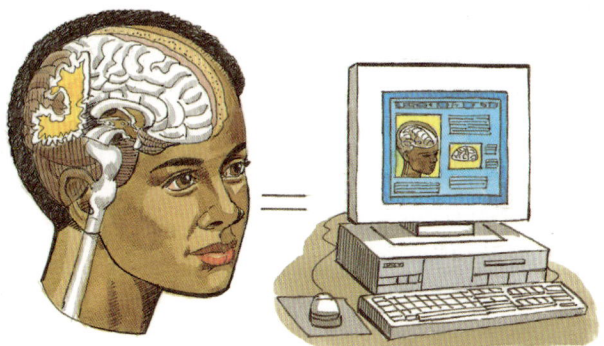

The brain works like a computer.
It collects, stores, sorts and sends information to other parts of the body.
Your brain controls almost everything that you do.

All animals have brains.
However, the human brain is more developed.
That is the reason human beings can do things that other animals cannot do.

Here are some pictures of animals showing their brain sizes compared to the size of their bodies.

The human brain weighs about 3 pounds or 1.4 kilograms.
A whale's brain weighs about 20 pounds or 9 kilograms.

How much heavier than a human brain is a whale's brain?
If you said about 17 pounds you would be correct.
17 pounds is about 7.6 kilograms.

Bar graphs

Graphs can be used to show the relationship between different things.
We can use a bar graph to tell about the weight of different animals.

Here are the weights of four animals on a farm.
The **cow** weighs 90 kilograms.
The **pig** weighs 40 kilograms.
The **goat** weighs 30 kilograms.
The **fowl** weighs 2 kilograms.

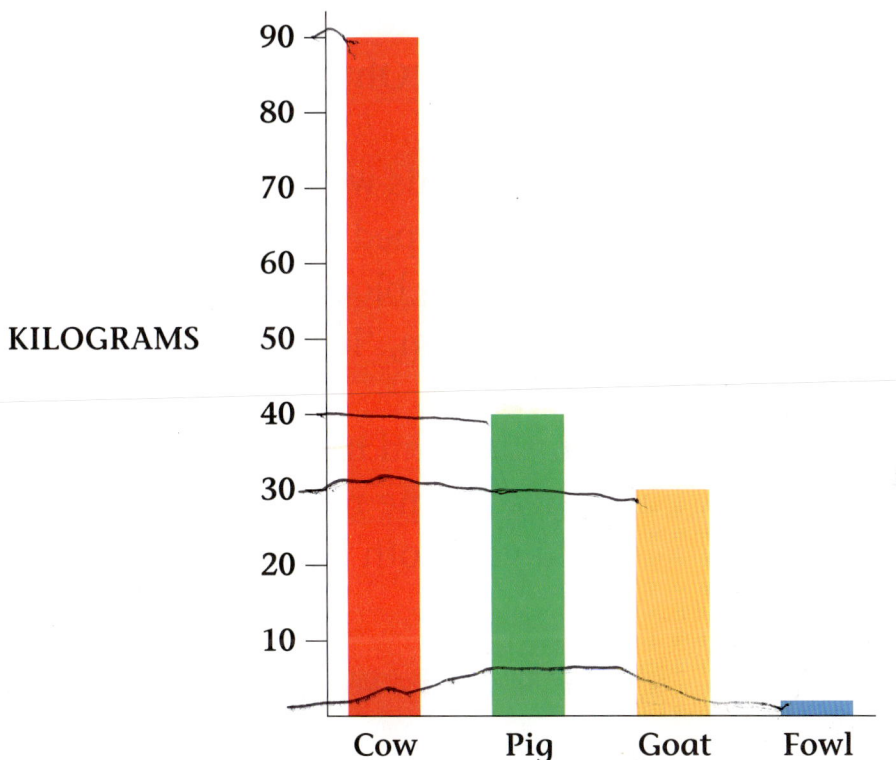

Let us talk about the information on this bar graph.
Which animal is the heaviest?
Which animal is the lightest?
Which animal weighs 40 kilograms?
Which animal weighs less than the pig but more than the fowl?

How do these parts work together?

2.1 Body parts working together

Read this story.

Story: **I am the Most Important**

One night Jo-Jo went to bed and she had a very bad dream.

She dreamt that there was a quarrel between her brain, heart and skeleton.

The brain shouted, 'Oh I am so happy, I am the most important.'

'Why do you feel this way?' asked the heart.

'Have you ever stopped to think what would happen if I stopped sending blood all over the body?'

'Well,' said the brain, 'If I am dead, how would you work?'

The skeleton that had been quiet all along shouted, 'Be quiet, I need some rest! I am the most important. Where would you both be if I was not around to shelter you?'

This made the brain and heart think.
The brain and heart shouted together, 'What value is a skeleton without a brain and a heart?'
At this point Jo-Jo had to say something. In a soft voice she said, 'Please, no more arguments, I need you all. You are all very important.
And we all need each other.'
Jo-Jo awoke about 8 o'clock next morning. She was happy to find that it was only a dream. She told Tammy and Gordon and they all had a good laugh.

Now that you have read the story 'I am the Most Important', whose side are you on?
Who do you think was correct?

> Discuss what you think with your friends.

The heart

The human heart is the strongest muscle in the body. It is our blood pumping muscle and it moves all the time to keep us breathing.
The heart pushes blood through our veins to send energy and oxygen to all parts of the body.

You can't *see* your heart working because it is in your rib cage.
You can *feel* it working.
Can you feel the beat?

You can feel the movement of your heart but you cannot feel the heart itself because it is protected by the rib cage.

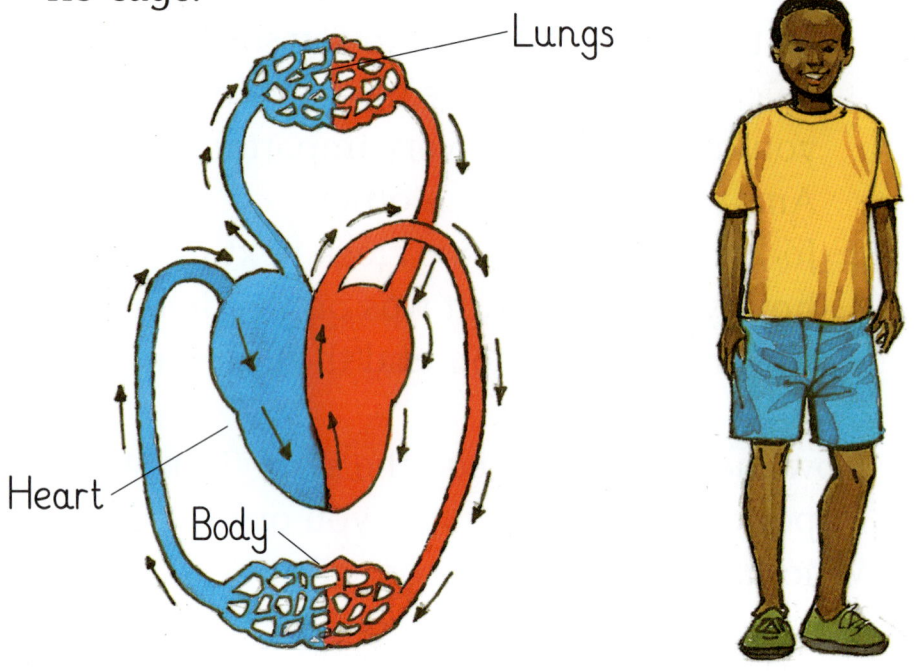

The blend sk

Blends are formed when two letters in a word give two different sounds.

When we say the words

    skeleton   **skin**   **skit**

we hear two separate sounds for 'sk'.
'sk' at the beginning of the word is called an *initial blend*.

Look at the pictures and say the words.
They all begin with the 'sk' initial blend.

sky   skip   skirt   skunk

skate   sketch   skull

Read this sentence aloud then put your finger on each initial blend and say the word again.

Skinny Skyler skipped and skated skilfully in her skimpy skirt.

Capital letters

Capital letters are used to begin sentences and special names.

Special names can be names of persons such as

Brenda   Mrs Whittaker   Miss Winsome   Paul   Mr Dennis

Special names can also be names of places

Kingston   Linstead   America   Dunns River   Workers' Bank

Page 49

The days of the week and the months of the year are also special names.

Days	Months
Sunday	January
Monday	February
Tuesday	March
Wednesday	April
Thursday	May
Friday	June
Saturday	July
	August
	September
	October
	November
	December

Look at this sentence.

> Mr Jones reminded Kenny to wear his helmet when he went riding at Emancipation Park on the first Sunday in June.

Read aloud all the special names in this sentence.
Say why they are special.

2.2 Writing about movement

Poem: **Body Movement**

My head I nod as the music starts
Moving it to the beat of my heart.
As the sweet music fills the air,
My moving body forgets its fear.
Sweet reggae songs loudly I sing,
While my ankles and knees do their thing.
My whole body moves to this wonderful beat,
Come let us dance in the burning heat.

Winnifred Whittaker

Full stops

We put full stops at the end of every telling sentence. A telling sentence makes a statement.

Oh yes, we also use full stops to show where words are shortened.

Read this passage and look at how the full stops are used.

Mr M. and Mrs W. Thomas took their children Joe and Maie to visit Sue in the U.S.A. in August. Sue took everyone to Disney Land. They had a great time. They watched the dolphins as they flipped over and over in the water. Sue said that she planned to go to the U.K. next year.

Let us look at the pictures and talk about what is happening.

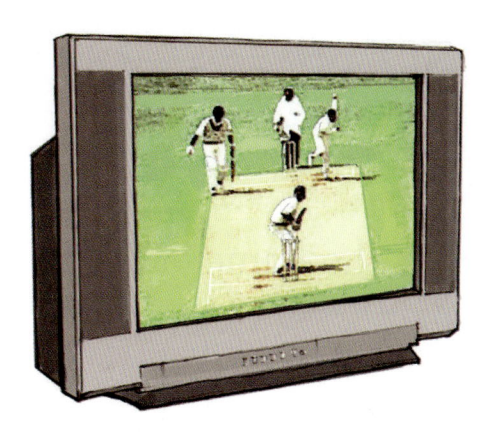

The England v. West Indies cricket match is on T.V. today.

Pauline is riding her bicycle.

The children are jumping rope.

The puppy is playing with a sack.

You should notice that each sentence begins with a capital letter and ends with a full stop.
Some parts of words have full stops as well. This is because these words are shortened.

Long Aa sound in word families

The letter 'a' in the words

    shake   **date**   **wage**

makes a long sound.

The long sound 'Aa' says the name of the letter 'Aa'.

Look at the pictures and say the words.

    cake   gate   cage

Let us read this sentence.

> Mother is late but she will bake a cake as soon as she comes through the gate and counts her wages.

Pick out the words with the long 'a' sound.

If you picked the words

    late   **bake**   **cake**   **gate**   **wages**

Then you are right.

These words also end with the word families '**ake**' '**ate**' and '**age**'.

Now make up your own sentence with words that have the long 'a' sound. The words must end with '**ake**' '**ate**' and '**age**'.

Sets

Sets can be described as groups of things.
Some sets have one member, while others may have many members.
There are also some sets that have no members.

Here is a set of eyes.

We can say that this is a set of two eyes.

Here is a set of fingers.

We can say that this is a set of ten fingers.

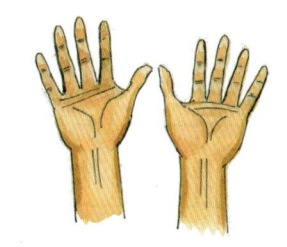

We can also group other body parts into sets.
Look at the pictures and read each sentence.

A set of two ears. 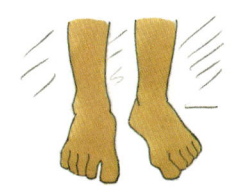   A set of ten toes. 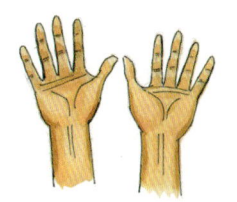   A set of two hands. 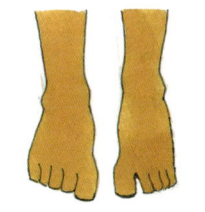   A set of two feet.

Sets can also be made up of things that are not related to the body.

A set of twelve oranges.    A set of four cars. 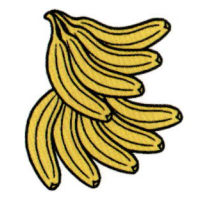   A set of nine bananas.    A set of five pencils.

2.3 Noisy bodies

Look at these pictures and talk about them.
Do the actions that are taking place in each one.

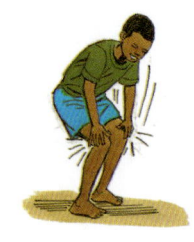

It's time to work in a group.
Get in a group and decide on an action. Perform the action.
Ask your teacher to help you decide on a song for your group. Do the action as the group sings the song.

The comma

Commas are used to separate the names of three or more things.

Read this passage. Look where the commas are.

Miss Peggy sells mangoes, oranges, plums, bananas and grapes at the school gate. After work she comes home, puts her shoes away, rests and then cooks dinner.

Look at this picture.

Say what you can see in the picture. If you were writing this down where would you put commas?

If we were talking about different body parts in one sentence we would have to use a comma to separate each word. Here is a sentence about the body.

My arms, legs, hands, feet, nose, ears and head are all parts of my body.

Mathematical symbols

There are some mathematical symbols that tell when a number is more than, less than or equal to another number. These are the symbols.

Symbol	Meaning
>	more than
<	less than
=	the same or equal to

The number of toes is more than the number of ears.
We can write this as:

number of toes > number of ears

The number of eyes is less than the number of fingers.
We can write this as:

number of eyes < number of fingers

The number of ears is equal to the number of eyes.
We can write this as:

number of ears = number of eyes

Using mathematical symbols

Look at these number sentences using symbols.

Number sentence		Word sentence
8 > 3	means	Eight is more than three.
4 = 2 + 2	means	Four is equal to two add two.
6 < 9	means	Six is less than nine.

Do you agree with these sentences?

Which symbol should be placed between each of these numbers?

12 ......?...... 5   17 ......?...... 21   16 ......?...... 8 + 8

2.4 Fit bodies

How do you keep fit?

People keep fit by doing different things.
Some go to the gym to exercise.
Others walk, jog or do jumping jacks.

Some children like to do frog leaps.
Some children stretch with their friends.

Find a safe activity to keep you fit.

Staying fit helps to keep your body healthy.

A healthy body makes a healthy mind.

Shapes

When we exercise, our bodies create shapes. The patterns can be curved, straight or twisted.

Here are some of the shapes that our bodies can make.

Stretching to one side.

Curling over like a letter C.

Lying straight.

Curled up in a ball.

We can also use our hands and feet to make shapes.

Talk about the shapes you can use your body parts to make.

More about shapes

The objects we see around us are different shapes.

triangle

rectangle

square

circle

Look around you. Find some objects that are these shapes. Say their names.

You can make these shapes with your bodies.

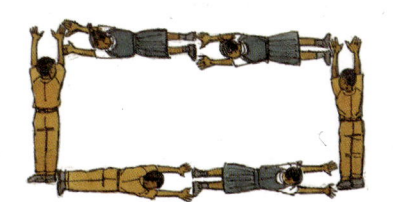

Making shapes such as triangles and rectangles.

Page 61

Sentence construction

When we write sentences we must begin with a capital letter. We can end with a full stop or question mark.

Telling sentences end with a full stop. These are sometimes called *statements*.

Mr Jones is wearing a straw hat.

Asking sentences end with a question mark. These are sometimes called *questions*.

Where is Marsha going today?

Read the sentences and say if each one is a telling sentence or an asking sentence.

I love to dance and sing.
Do you like ring games?
A triangle has three sides.
How many sides does a square have?
Is grandma arriving in the morning or the afternoon?
It will be dark before father gets home from work.

2.5 How animals move

Have you ever watched animals moving?

Animals move in different ways.
Some move slowly while others move swiftly.
Here are pictures of some animals on the move.
Let us look at them and talk about how they move.

The fish are swimming through the water.

The frogs are jumping to the pond.

The birds are flying in the air between the trees.

The lizards are crawling up the wall.

Use your body to move like these animals.

Page 63

Moving along

Poem: **Moving**

Fish swim swiftly in the rushing waters
Watched by enemies all around.
Birds fly high in the clear blue sky
Searching for food as they pass by.
Snakes slither silently in search for food
Hoping that frogs are in a sleepy mood.
From their hiding place, with open eyes
Sit speckled toads ready to eat juicy flies.

Winnifred Whittaker

3 How do we differ in size?

3.1 Tall and short

Comparing people and objects

Tom

Tim

Tom and Tim are friends. They go everywhere together.

Tom is tall. He can reach books from the top shelf of the library.

Tim is short. He can reach books from the bottom shelf of the library.

Tall and **short** are two words we use to *compare* people or objects.

Think of other words used to compare people or objects.

Alike and different

Look at the picture.

Samantha

Suzan

Page 66

We can compare Samantha and Suzan by saying how they are alike and how they are different.

We can say that Samantha and Suzan are alike because they are girls.
We can say they are different because Samantha is taller than Suzan.

Discuss the picture with the person next to you.
Say some other ways in which the girls are alike and ways in which they are different.

More about comparing

We can compare other things by how they are alike and how they are different.

Look at these pictures and talk about them.

Page 67

Estimating measurement

When we *estimate* measurement we make a guess about it.

Look at Josann's name tag and estimate how long it is.

JOSANN

Josann's name tag is about 3 cm long.

Here are some things that you will find in your classroom.

pencil   chair leg   foot   book   stick of chalk

finger   arm   chalkboard   door   plant

Let us look at these things and estimate their measurements.

What are your estimates?

Now use a ruler or metre stick to find out the true measurement.
Compare your estimates with the true measurements.

3.2 Measuring height and weight

Body measurement

We might estimate or guess someone's weight or their height.
We can tell their *exact* weight or height by using the correct measuring instrument.

To measure length, height or width, use a ruler or metre stick.
These measurements will be in centimetres.

Page 69

To measure your weight you need a *scale*.
These measurements will be in grams and kilograms.
There are different types of scales.

Look carefully at the scales in the pictures.

Discuss what each scale is used for weighing.

Heavy or light?

This is a simple arm balance.
It can help us tell which is the heavier of two things.
It cannot tell the exact weight.

The bigger mango is heavier, so the weight pushes down one arm of the balance.
The lighter side goes up.

Here are two ackee. They are the same weight.

The ackees are placed one on each side of the arm balance.
Say what happens.

One of the ackees is taken away.
Say what happens.

Netball

Read this passage.

Netball is a team game. It is played by a team of seven players. A team is a group. Each person in the group has a job to do. Each player wears a bib. It tells the job that she has to do and the places on court that she can play. The group has a leader. She is the captain. The game has rules. Members of the group must obey the rules.

3.3 Measuring bones

Using a ruler to measure bones

Have you ever thought about measuring your bones?
Bones are all over your body.
When you look at the skeleton you will notice that all bones are not the same length.

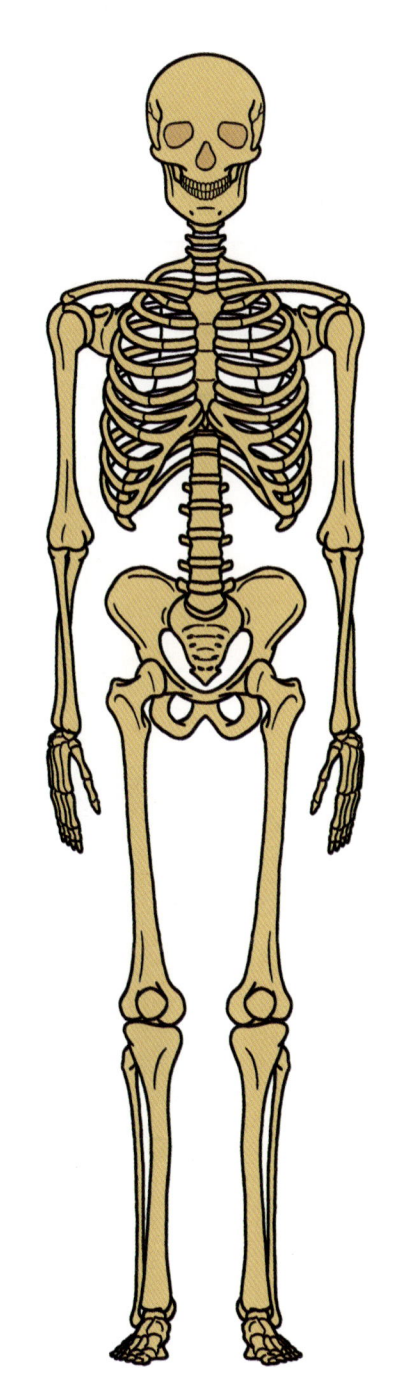

Some bones are long and some are short.
Some bones are also broad.

We need a ruler to measure our bones.

Get a partner to work with you.
Measure the bones in both of your hands and feet and write down the measurement.

When you have measured all the bones compare the lengths of your partner's bones with yours.
Whose bones are longer?

Comparing lengths

Bones in the body can be compared by their length: how long or how short they are.
Other things around us can also be compared by their lengths.

Look at these pictures and discuss them. Which object in each set is longer?

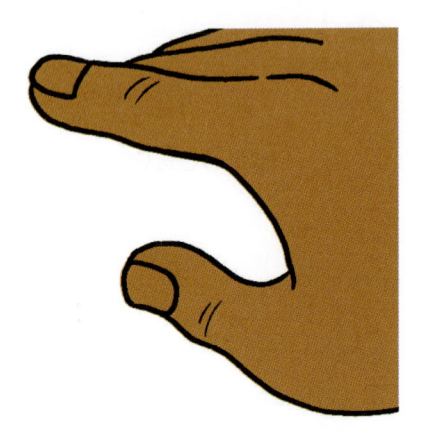

finger and thumb

plantain and banana

ruler and pen

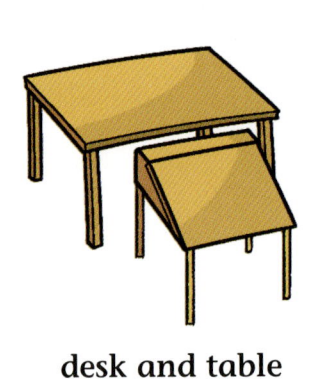

desk and table

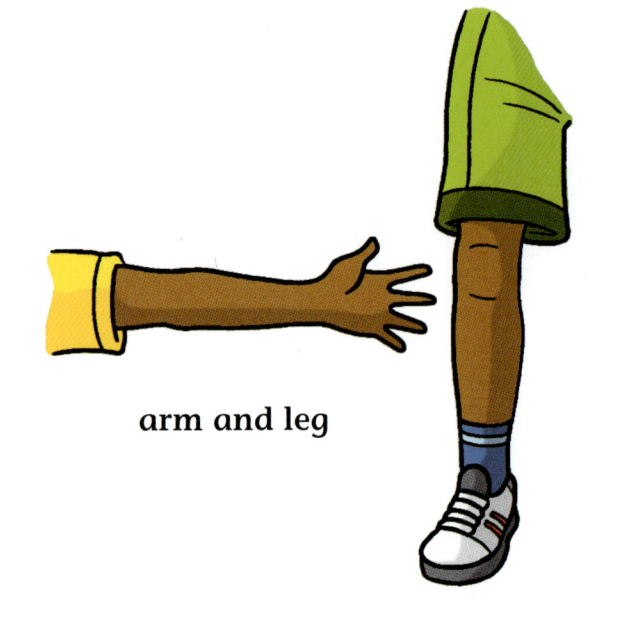

arm and leg

Comparing lengths using graphs

If we wanted to compare the lengths of the feet of six children, we could use a bar graph.

The children are

Tonia   Marcus   Kahlil   Suzy   Winnie   Kadie

Their foot measurements are:
- Tonia   20 centimetres
- Marcus   26 centimetres
- Kahlil   30 centimetres
- Suzy   19 centimetres
- Winnie   25 centimetres
- Kadie   20 centimetres

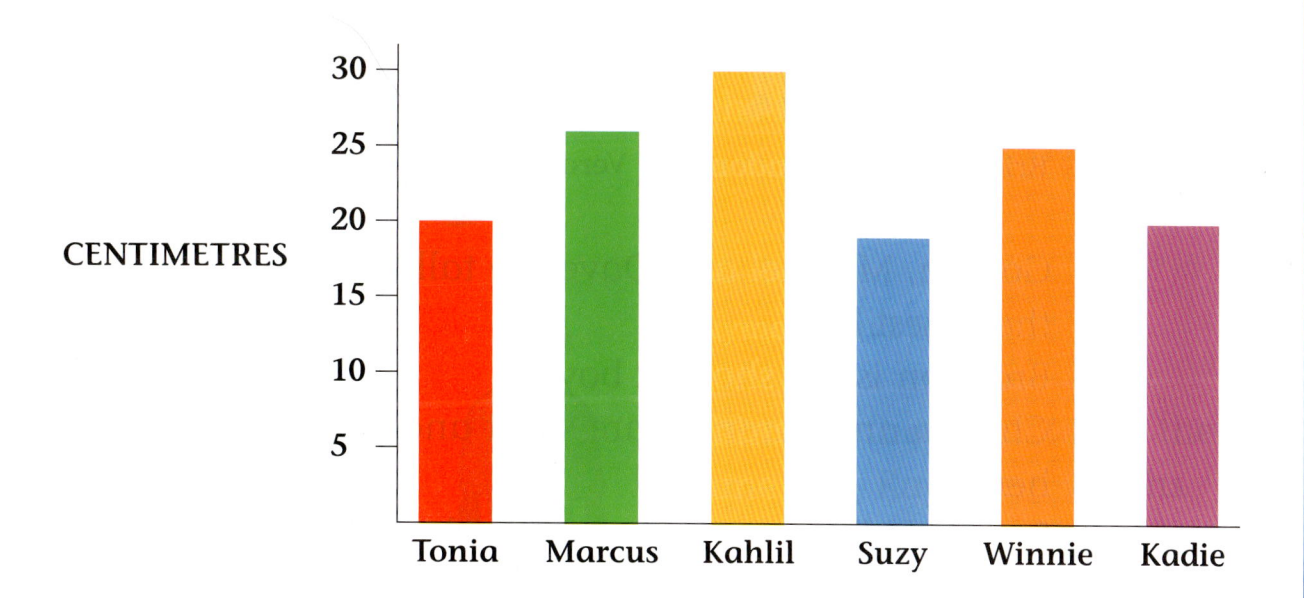

This bar graph tells us that Kahlil has the longest foot and Suzy has the shortest.

> Talk about the lengths of Tonia's foot and Winnie's foot.

Page 75

Using symbols to compare weights

We can use the symbols < and > to compare weights.

Do you remember what they mean?

< means less than   > means more than

40 kg < 50 kg   so Patra is lighter than Zona.
45 kg > 40 kg   so Raymond is heavier than Delroy.

Opposites

Sometimes when people or things are not the same we say they are *opposites*.

Here are some opposites.

Use the pictures to help you say the words.

Word		Opposite	
little		big	
boy		girl	
up		down	

straight   crooked

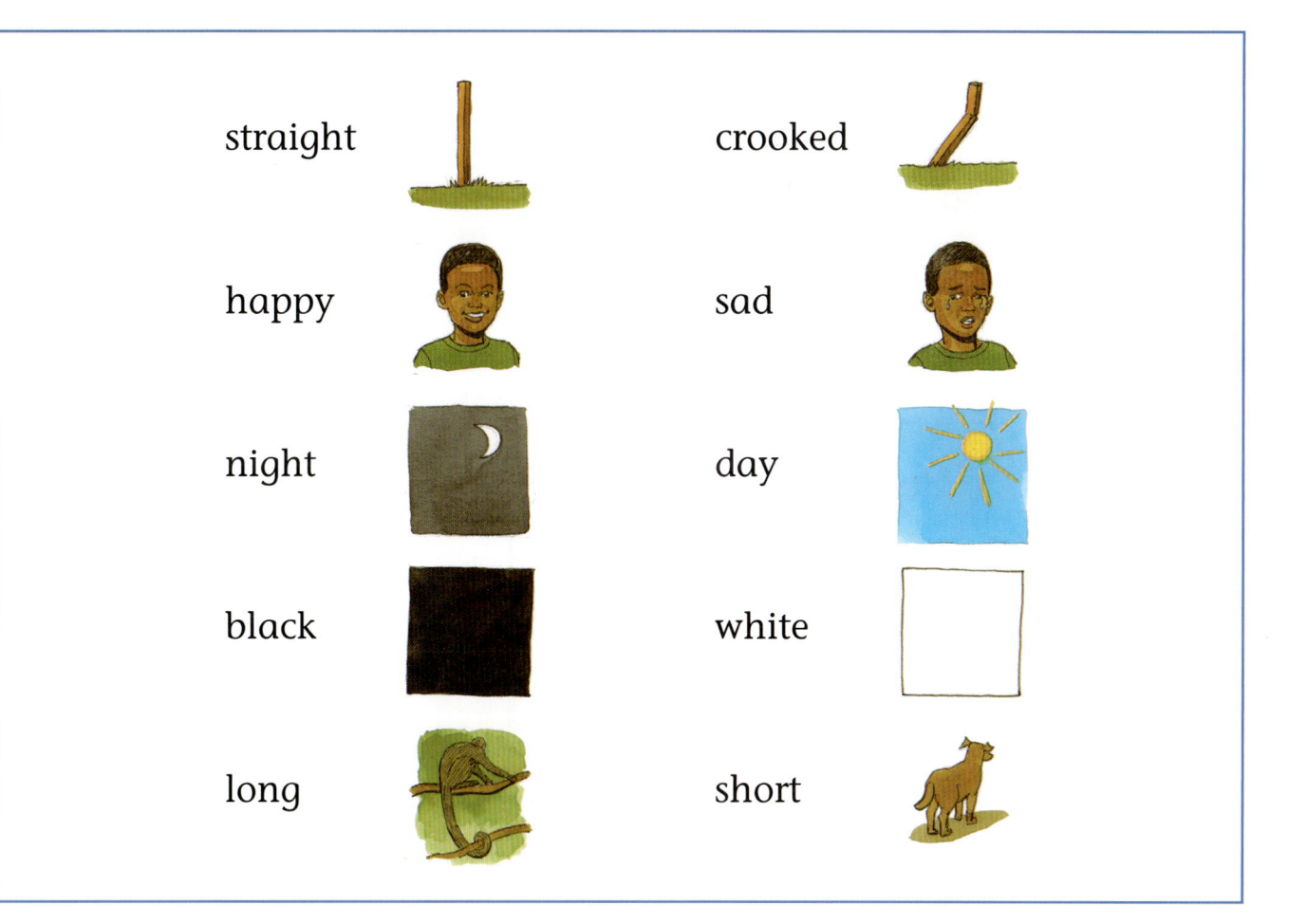

happy   sad

night   day

black   white

long   short

More about opposites

Here are two groups of students having lunch.

Say the words for things in the picture that are opposites.

Pairs or sets

Did you know that almost all the bones in your body come in *pairs* or sets?
A pair means two of something.

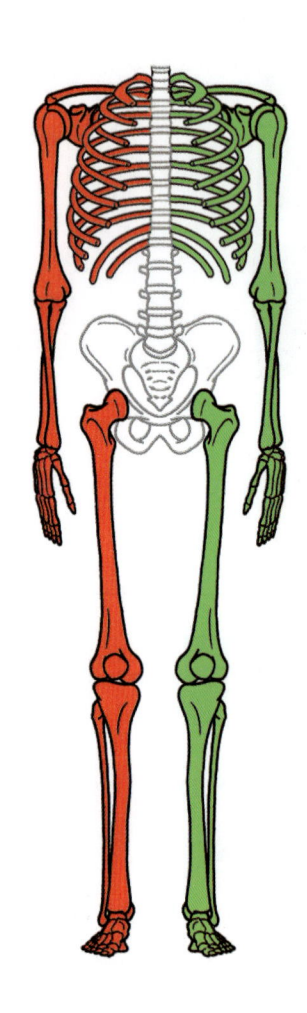

Look at the positions of the bones on the skeleton.
Can you match which ones are paired to each other?

Let us count the bones in the rib cage.
How many did you get?

If you got 24 in all, then you are right.
There are 12 on one side and 12 on the other side.

3.5 Size and sound

The sounds that animals make are sometimes related to their sizes.
Some small animals make soft sounds.
Some large animals make loud sounds.

Look at these animals and talk about the sounds they make.

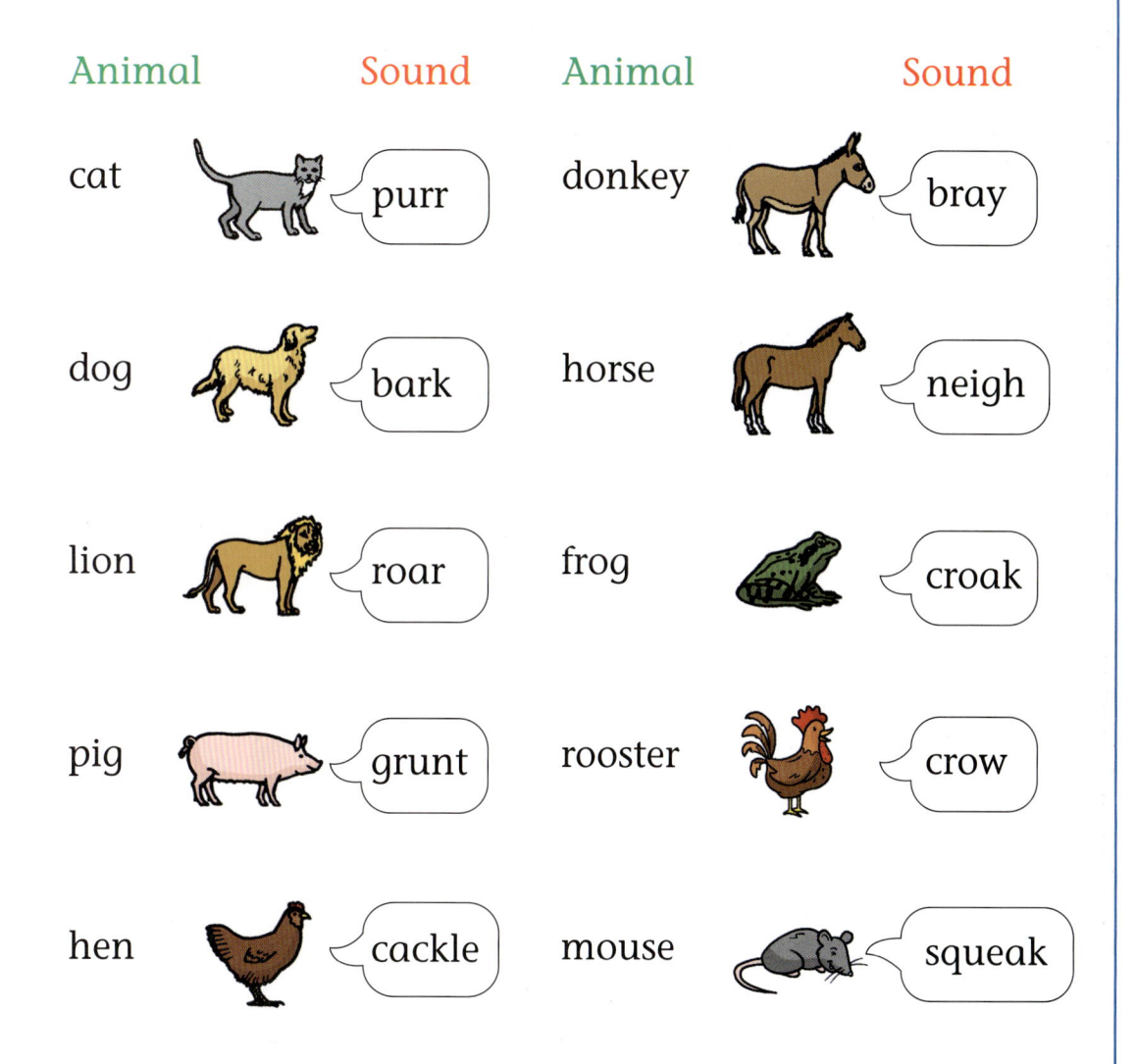

Animal	Sound	Animal	Sound
cat	purr	donkey	bray
dog	bark	horse	neigh
lion	roar	frog	croak
pig	grunt	rooster	crow
hen	cackle	mouse	squeak

Imitate the sound made by each of the animals in the picture.

Which of these is your favourite sound? Say why.

Page 81

Comparing size

Size is how big or how small an object or thing is.

A cat is **smaller** so it makes a **softer** sound than a dog.

When we want to compare two things we can add 'er' to a describing word.

Look at this boy and his dog.

Use these describing words to compare them.

tall   short   fat   small   big   smart   noisy   quiet

Talk about this picture with your friends. Use size words to compare things.

3.6 How animals move

The animals are lined up for a race to see who is fastest.

Each animal is tagged with a number.

Number	Competitor
1	dog
2	cat
3	frog
4	turtle
5	goat
6	horse
7	snail

Which animal do you think will finish first?

Which animal do you think will finish last?

These animals ran a fair race and this is how they finished.

Were you surprised at where any animal finished?
If your answer is yes explain why.

Ordinal numbers

Ordinal numbers are used to tell the order or *position* in a series or group of things.

In the animal race, there were seven animals. They finished the race in different positions from first to seventh.

Here is the way we write the first twenty positions. They can also be written in a short form.

Position	Short form	Position	Short form
first	1st	eleventh	11th
second	2nd	twelfth	12th
third	3rd	thirteenth	13th
fourth	4th	fourteenth	14th
fifth	5th	fifteenth	15th
sixth	6th	sixteenth	16th
seventh	7th	seventeenth	17th
eighth	8th	eighteenth	18th
ninth	9th	nineteenth	19th
tenth	10th	twentieth	20th

Movement of animals

Animals move in different ways.

Animal	Movement
fish	swims
snail	crawls
snake	slithers
horse	gallops
frog	leaps

Move like each of these animals.

Use your mouth to make sounds to match each movement.
Repeat the movements and make the sounds.

Name some other animals and say how they move.

3.7 David and Goliath

Read this story.

Story: **Size against Strength: the Fight of David and Goliath**

Long ago in the days when the Bible was written there lived a big, strong giant man named Goliath. He was a warrior and fought many battles. One day he decided to fight a little shepherd boy named David. David was not afraid of Goliath and so he agreed to fight him.

Everyone laughed at David and thought he could not win the fight. Goliath was armed with a spear, a sword and a shield. David had only a sling shot that fired stones.

Goliath and David fought and David won the fight. He used his sling shot and stones to defeat Goliath.

You can also read this story in the Bible in Samuel 1: 17.

Let us sing a song about David.

Song: **Boy Named David**

>Only a boy named David
>Only a rippling brook
>Only a boy named David
>Five little stones he took
>And one little stone went in the sling
>And the sling went round and round
>And the sling went round and round
>Oh! Round and round and round and round and round
>One little prayer went up to God
>And the giant came tumbling down.

3.8 Muscles

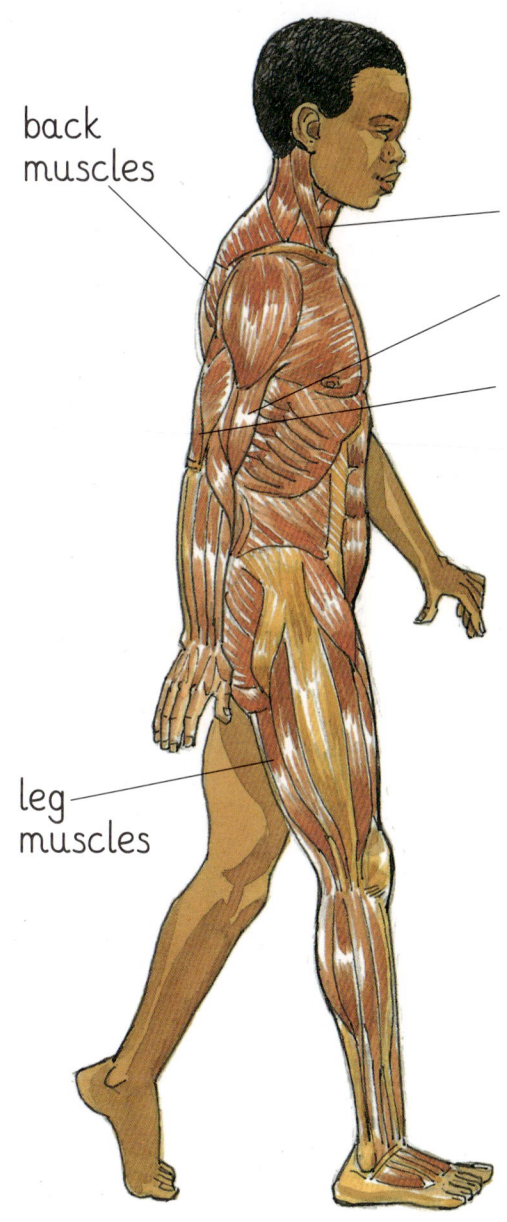

- back muscles
- neck muscles
- arm muscles (biceps)
- arm muscles (triceps)
- leg muscles

Muscles help your body move. Muscles work even when you are not moving about.
Every time you blink or breathe your muscles work.

You can control the muscles in your arms and legs. You can move them about or keep them still. The largest and strongest muscles in your body are in your legs. They help you walk, squat and stand on tiptoes.
They also keep you steady when you stand still.

There are some muscles that you cannot control. These include your stomach muscles, which help you digest food. They also include your heart muscles, which pump blood around your body.

Muscles and exercise

Exercise strengthens muscles and keeps them working well.

When you exercise, your muscles become toned and fit.

People who do not exercise become tired more easily. Their muscles become weak.

4 How do I keep my body healthy?

4.1 Grouping foods

The foods we eat

Food helps to keep our bodies healthy.
Our bodies need different kinds of food.
We need food to make us **go**, **glow** and **grow**.

Go foods

Glow foods

Grow foods

A *balanced* meal should have foods from all three food groups.
If we do not eat foods from all the food groups our diet will be *unbalanced*.
An unbalanced diet may cause us to be tired or weak. It may prevent us from being active.

Linking foods to groups

We can put different kinds of food into groups or sets. Here are some groups of foods.

Staples

Legumes

Fruits

Proteins

Vegetables

Fats

Page 92

Sets

There are things you already know about sets.

- A set is a group of things.
- A set may have one member or many members.
- A set may have no members.

Let us look at some sets.

This is a set of vegetables.

This is a set of fruits.

We can also have sets with one kind of fruit and one kind of vegetable.

A set of 6 oranges.

A set of 5 carrots.

A set of 8 apples.

A set of 4 cabbages.

The letter Ff

The letter 'Ff' makes the sound you hear at the beginning of the words:

food   family   father   female   fan   fern

Call out these words.

The letter 'Ff' also makes the beginning sound you hear when you say the names of these pictures.

Look at the pictures and say the words.

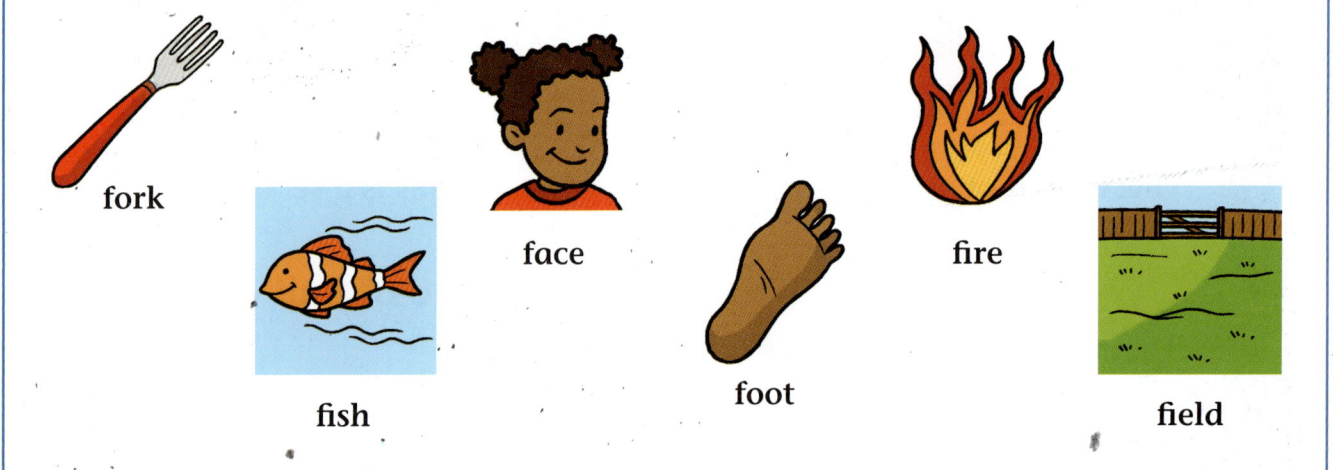

fork

fish

face

foot

fire

field

Here is a passage. Which of these words should go in each space?
Read the passage and call out the right word for each space.

> Mr Jones caught a … in the river. He decided to cook it and eat it with a knife and ….. . He made a …. in the corner of the …. . As he was collecting sticks he caught his …. on the root of a tree and tripped over. He hit his …. on a stone but he was not badly hurt.

4.2 Eating right

We must eat the right kinds of food to stay healthy.

Some people will only eat food from groups they like. They leave food from other groups that they don't like. For example, they might like fruits but not vegetables.

If we don't eat vegetables we will not get some of the important nutrients they need to keep healthy.

We should eat foods from several groups in every meal.

Breakfast

Lunch

Dinner

Here are some important words you should know.

			E	N	E	R	G	Y		
		S	T	A	P	L	E	S		
	P	R	O	T	E	I	N			
			D	I	S	E	A	S	E	
				N	U	T	R	I	T	I	O	N
			V	E	G	E	T	A	B	L	E
					☺					
				F	R	U	I	T		
				D	I	E	T			
			L	E	G	U	M	E	S	
				H	E	A	L	T	H	Y
				F	A	T	S			

Call out each word.

What time do we eat?

Breakfast is the first meal of the day. Some people have that meal about 7 o'clock in the morning.

Look at the clock faces and tell the times that we have our meals.

7 o'clock
breakfast

12 o'clock
lunch

5 o'clock
dinner

Page 96

Sometimes we do things at particular times.
Look at the clock faces and tell the time that each activity is done.

8 o'clock
school starts

10 o'clock
break time

3 o'clock
school dismisses

Name 3 other activities you do on a Saturday or a Sunday.
Tell the time you do them.

Describing food

Adjectives are describing words. They tell us more about naming words (nouns).

Read the adjectives that describe each of these foods.

delicious

crispy

hot

spicy

Page 97

soft
juicy
ripe
sweet

flat
round
crumbly
dry

Think about other words that could describe the foods that you eat.
Share them with the rest of the class.

4.3 Menu making

A menu is a list of dishes that we can choose from.
Look at this menu. Say what you would choose.

Marlon's Saturday Menu

Breakfast
cereal
fruit juice
toast and eggs
milk

Lunch
patty
cheese sandwich
rice and sardine
lemonade

Snacks
fresh fruits
crackers and cheese
cookies and milk
dried fruits

Dinner
vegetable soup
ackee and saltfish
boiled yam
steamed vegetables

Making a recipe

A *recipe* is a list of things needed to make a drink or meal.
The recipe also tells you how to make the drink or meal.

Here is the recipe for making lemonade:

Recipe for making lemonade

Here is what you need:
1 litre water
$\frac{1}{2}$ cup sugar
3 lemons

Here is what you do:
1   Put the sugar in a large jug.
2   Pour the water into the jug with the sugar.
3   Add the lemon juice.
4   Stir until the sugar is dissolved.
5   Pour into glasses and add ice.

If we add cherry to the recipe the drink could be called cherryade.
Think of something you would add to the recipe. What would you call your drink?

We can estimate how many there are by looking.

Estimate the weight of these items.

2 fingers of green bananas

3 head of cabbage

6 Irish potatoes

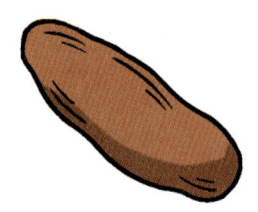

1 piece of yam

1 breadfruit

More than one – plural with 'es' ending

We have looked at adding 's' to the ends of some words to make them plural.
Here are some more examples.

bird   birds    apple   apples    banana   bananas

For some words we must add 'es' to make them plural. We speak of **one bus** but **two buses**.

Here are some other words that add 'es' to the end to make them plural.

box   boxes    dish   dishes    fish   fishes

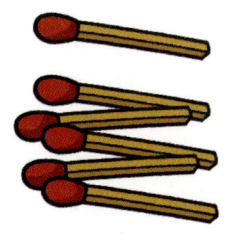

match   matches    glass   glasses    watch   watches

Page 105

4.5 Buying food

The supermarket

Read this passage about Big Tree Supermarket.

This is Big Tree Supermarket. Many people shop here. It is large and clean. Mother says the workers are polite and helpful. Sometimes I go to the supermarket with mother. I help her to push the trolley.

I love to visit the fruit counter.
My favourite fruits are bananas and mangoes. Can you see my favourite fruits on the counter?

4.6 Religion and food

Are all kinds of foods eaten by all religious groups?

In Jamaica and all over the world some religious groups do not eat some kinds of food.

Some religions have rules about foods.
The rules say what foods members should eat.
They also say what foods members should not eat.

In the Jewish religion people eat beef, lamb and venison. They also eat fish that have scales and fins. Some foods that they don't eat are shellfish, crab, lobster and food from pigs.

Muslims are not allowed to eat food from pigs or drink alcohol.

Among Christians, Seventh Day Adventists do not eat food from pigs.

Another group that does not eat food from pigs is the Rastafarians. They consider it unclean. Some Rastafarians eat fish while others eat no meat at all.

Long Oo sound

Look at the pictures and say the words.

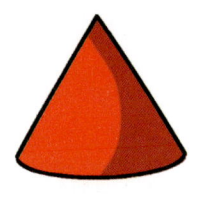

| cone | rose | bone | nose | hose | telephone |

Say these words again and listen to the sound of 'Oo' in each word.

What can you say about the sound of the 'Oo' in each word?

The long sound of 'Oo' says the name of the letter 'O'.

> Say some other words that have the long sound of 'Oo'.

4.7 The vegetarian

A *vegetarian* is a person who does not eat some or all food from animals.

Vegetarians have different reasons for not eating food from animals.

Some reasons are:
- religious belief
- they think slaughtering animals is cruel
- they believe that eating only food from plants is healthier
- they do not like animal flesh.

Strict vegetarians eat only vegetables, grains, fruits and nuts.

What's for dinner?

Mr Jones is a vegetarian. He buys his groceries at the health food store.
He buys fresh fruits and vegetables at the market.
Although Mr Jones is a vegetarian, he eats fish.
Today Mr Jones is preparing dinner.
Let us read what is on the menu.

Dinner menu for Mr Jones

Stewed peas and rice
Baked potatoes
Fried plantain
Steamed vegetables

Fruit punch

Here is Mr Jones enjoying his dinner.

Which of these foods do you like best?

Pronouns

We spoke about Mr Jones the vegetarian.
We can talk about Mr Jones without using his name.
Instead we can use the words 'he' and 'him'
The words 'he' and 'him' are called *pronouns*.

Pronouns are words that we use in place of nouns.

If we were talking about a woman, instead of using her name we could use the words 'she' or 'her' instead.
If we are talking about a thing, instead of using its name we could use the word 'it'.

Look at the following sentences.

Tom is kicking a ball
We can also say '**He** is kicking a ball'.

Mary is wearing a red dress.
We can also say '**She** is wearing a red dress'.

The **book** is on the table.
We can also say '**It** is on the table'.

4.8 Healthy body

We have only one body.
Don't you think we should make every effort to keep it safe and healthy?
It is very wise to practise good hygiene daily.
Here are some ways to practise good hygiene.

Bath every day and wear clean clothes.

Whenever possible brush your teeth after every meal.

Keep your hair well combed.

Store garbage in covered bins.

Cover foods to keep away germs carried by flies and other insects.

Wash fruits and vegetables before you eat them.

Page 111

Money – addition and subtraction

To keep healthy there are many goods and services that we must pay for.

It is important that we learn to calculate money so that we know how much to pay when we shop.

I buy a bottle of fruit drink for $20.00 and a sandwich for $10.00.
I do an addition like this to find out how much I am spending:

$$\begin{array}{r} \$20.00 \\ + \ \$10.00 \\ \hline \$30.00 \end{array}$$

So I am spending $30.00.

I hand in a $50.00 note to pay for my food.
I do a subtraction like this to find out how much change I need:

$$\begin{array}{r} \$50.00 \\ - \ \$30.00 \\ \hline \$20.00 \end{array}$$

So I receive $20.00 in change.

4.9 Healthy school

Children are sometimes absent from school because they are not well.
They may be suffering from an illness or a disease.

Some of the common diseases that affect children of all ages are measles, mumps and conjunctivitis, also known as 'pink eye'.

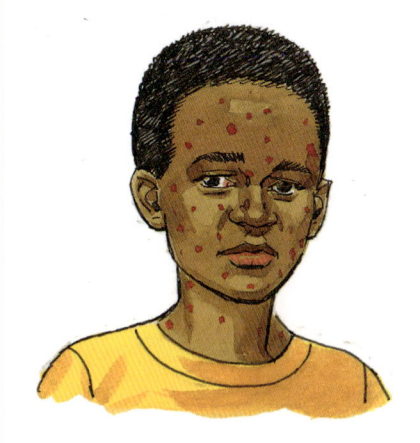

measles

mumps

'pink eye'

'Pink eye' is a common disease that affects both adults and children in Jamaica. It is also a disease that is spread from one person to another.

Children with 'pink eye' must stay away from school for at least ten days so that their classmates do not catch the disease from them.

Pictographs

This table tells us the number of students absent from six classes because of 'pink eye'.

Class	Number of students absent with 'pink eye'
Grade 1	3
Grade 2	5
Grade 3	6
Grade 4	4
Grade 5	2
Grade 6	4

We can show this information as a pictograph.
A pictograph shows information in a way that is easy to understand.

Class	Number of students absent with 'pink eye'
Grade 1	👤👤👤
Grade 2	👤👤👤👤👤
Grade 3	👤👤👤👤👤👤
Grade 4	👤👤👤👤
Grade 5	👤👤
Grade 6	👤👤👤👤

What does the pictograph tell us about the students in these classes?

It tells us the class that had the most students with 'pink eye'.
Which class was that?

It tells us the class that had the least students with 'pink eye'.
Which class was that?

It also tells us how many children in all the classes had 'pink eye'.
How many were there?

More about pictographs

Here is another pictograph.
It represents the number of books that six students read during the holidays

Student	Number of books read during the holidays
Susan	📖📖📖📖📖📖📖📖📖
Mary	📖📖📖📖📖
Robby	📖📖📖📖📖📖📖
Gary	📖📖📖
Nicole	📖📖📖📖📖📖
Adam	📖📖📖📖

Talk about this pictograph with the person next to you.
What information does it tell you?

Verbs adding 'ed'

Read this sentence.

    Children with 'pink eye' <u>stayed</u> away from school.

We add 'ed' to the word 'stay' to show that the action is not happening now but happened some time ago.

When 'ed' is added to some verbs the *past tense* is formed.

Here are some verbs to which we can add 'ed' to form the *past tense*.

play	**walk**	**wait**	**work**	**answer**	**show**
jump	**call**	**push**	**ask**	**snow**	**roll**

We can add 'ed' to each of these to tell about an action that we did some time ago.

    I played cricket last weekend.
    I walked to school yesterday.
    I waited for my friend last Saturday.

Say a sentence with each of the other words to tell about something you did some time ago.

4.10 Sounds and feelings

The ear

Can you imagine what our world would be like without sound?

For those of us who can hear, sound affects our daily lives in many ways.

Look at the diagram.
You will see that the ear has three parts.
The outer ear is the only part that we can actually see.

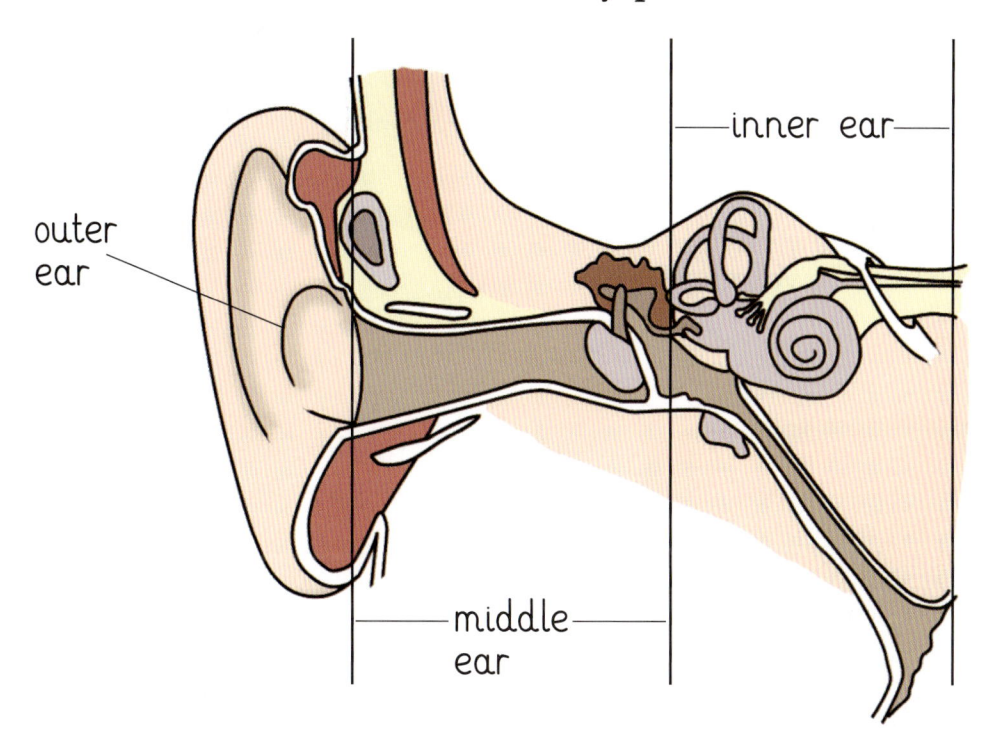

Say the names of the parts of the ear.

Taking care of your ears

You need to take good care of your ears.
Here are some things you should not do because they might damage your ears.

Never put anything sharp or pointed in your ears even if they are itchy. Pointed objects might pierce the eardrum.

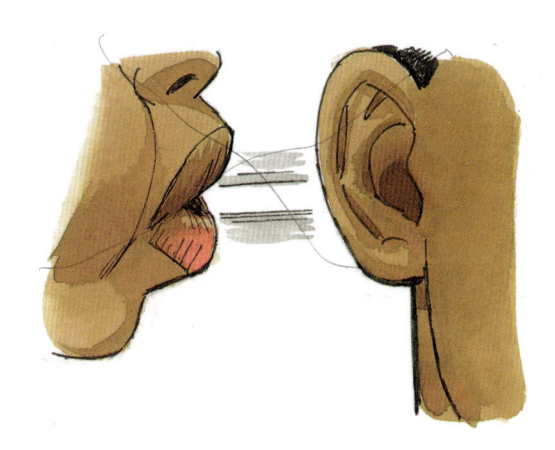

Don't allow anyone to shout or blow in your ears.

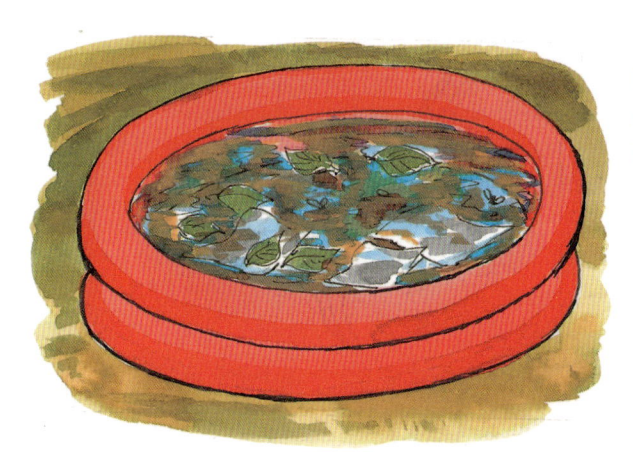

Never swim in dirty water because germs might get into your ears and cause an infection.

Don't blow your nose too hard when you have a cold.

4.11 Take a rest

The importance of rest

Eating the right foods and keeping the body clean are ways to stay healthy.
Rest and exercise are also a part of healthy living.
Did you know that animals as well as people need rest?

We do not need to sleep in order to rest.
There are different ways in which we can rest.

Say what is happening in these pictures.

Rest is just as important as work and play. At the end of the day your body is tired. Your body needs time to rest and prepare itself for the next day.

If you don't allow your body to relax and repair you will not become strong enough to continue to work and play the next day. You might be too tired to complete all your chores.

Talk with the person next to you about what might happen if you don't get enough rest.

Page 119

Jesus also needed rest

Read this story.

Story: **Jesus Calms the Storm**

Jesus had spent all day teaching the crowd and healing many sick people.
He was becoming very tired.

He said to his disciples, 'Let us go to the other side of the sea.'
The disciples sent away the large crowd and they got into a big boat with Jesus.
As they were sailing away they noticed that other small boats were following them and people were calling to them.

They were talking and laughing as they sailed. Suddenly a storm started and big waves began tossing the boat and filling it with water. While all this was going on Jesus was sleeping in the back of the boat.

His frightened friends woke Him and said, 'Master don't you care if we drown?'

Jesus got up immediately and began speaking sternly to the wind.

Then he said to the sea, 'Peace, be still.'

The storm stopped immediately, and the sea was calm again.

You can also read this story in the Bible in Matthew 8: 23–27.

Using verbs ending in -ing

In the story 'Jesus Calms the Storm' some of the words used were verbs ending in 'ing'.

Sometimes when a verb ends in 'ing' it tells us that action is taking place in the present.

Look at each of these pictures and read about the action that is taking place.

Paul is <u>climbing</u> the tree.

The cat is <u>sleeping</u> on the bed.

Mother is <u>watering</u> the flowers.

Miss is <u>teaching</u> a lesson.

Page 122

4.12 Animals at rest

Animals serve their masters in different ways.

Some animals protect us.

Some give us food.

Some are kept for sports.

Other animals like cats and dogs are kept as pets.
All animals need rest to keep them strong and healthy.
Animals that are kept working without rest times might get sick and die of tiredness.
Animals are our friends and we should show care by giving them time to rest.

How animals rest

Here are some animals at rest.
Let us read about what each one is doing.

The dog is lying on a rug.

The cat is sleeping on the sofa.

A donkey is grazing under a tree.

The cows are standing in the pasture.

Look at the pictures and say how these animals rest.
Talk about it with the person next to you.

Page 124

Don't

✗ Play in the street where there is traffic.

✗ Play with sharp knives.

✗ Play with matches.

✗ Run along the corridors.

✗ Play near open grids or pits.

✗ Take other peoples' medicines.

Look at this picture and talk about how people are using the road.

Page 129

Fire! Fire!

Read this story.

Story: **The Fire**

'Mama wake up! wake up!' shouted Sandra.
'What's the matter child?' called Mrs Black.
'The kitchen is on fire!' Sandra cried as Mrs Black ran from the house.

'Where is everyone? Are they all safe?' asked Mrs Black.
'Yes mama, I was the only one in here, May and Carl went to look for Miss Daisy.'
'O Lord! I didn't even call the fire brigade,' cried Mrs Black.
'Don't worry mama, I called them. Hear the siren, they are close by.'

'How did this happen, Sandra?' asked her mama.
'I was cooking and the curtains caught alight,' said Sandra. She burst into tears.
'Look! Look at her hands, they are burnt,' cried Mrs Black. 'Help me take her to the hospital.'

Read the story again. Discuss keeping safe from fire with the person next to you.

Making sentences

A sentence is a group of words that are put together to tell us something.

Let us read these sentences.

The boy rides a bike.

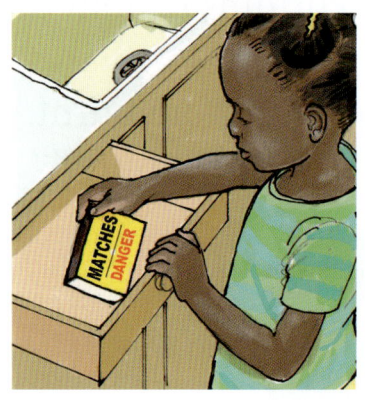

Sandra puts matches away safely.

In each of these sentences there is a naming part and a telling or doing part.

The boy is the naming part of the sentence, because it tells us who is doing something.

rides a bike is the telling part of the sentence, it tells us what somebody is doing.

Sandra is the naming part of the sentence.

puts matches away safely is the telling part of the sentence.

More about sentences

Look at these pictures and make your own sentences.

Identify the naming part and the telling part in each of your sentences.

Safety on the road

Some people drive cars on the roads. Others ride bicycles or walk.
People who walk on the roads are called *pedestrians*.

Everyone must practise safety on the roads.

You should always wear a seat belt.

You should always wear a helmet.

You should always look each way before crossing the road.

Tell your friend two ways you practise safety on the road.

5.2 Accidents in the home

Safety at home

Accidents happen in the home all the time.
Accidents are sometimes caused by carelessness.

Accidents in the home can be prevented if rules are obeyed.
Obeying rules will keep us safe from harm or danger.
There are things that we can do at home to keep ourselves safe.

Here are some of the things that we can do.

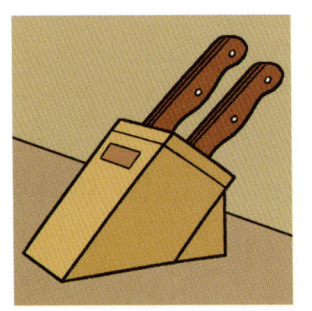

✓ Knives and sharp objects should be kept out of the reach of children.

✓ The handles of pots should be turned in when on the stove.

✓ Cuts and bruises should be cleaned and covered.

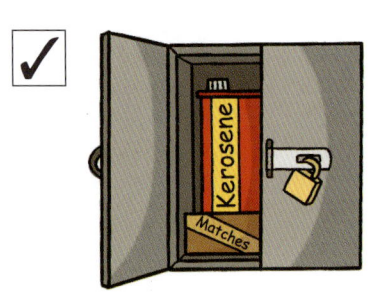

✓ Matches and kerosene should be kept in secure places.

✓ Chemicals used for cleaning, such as bleach, should be put away in a safe place.

> Listening and safety

Read this story.

Story: **Bouncing Brenda**

Brenda was brilliant and she liked to bounce balls as she moved. She seldom ever walked, and so she was nicknamed 'Bouncing Brenda'.
She was very bright and she always did her homework. However, she had a problem.
She loved to swing on the branches of the trees in her big open yard.

Her mother was sure that one day she might hurt herself, so she begged her to be careful.
Brenda did not listen to her.
She thought that if she fell she would only get a small bruise, and that would heal quickly.
On a bright Tuesday afternoon Brenda rushed outside to swing.
To her this was the most enjoyable thing to do.
The evening was calm. A breeze was blowing gently.

Page 135

Brenda grasped her favourite branch, gave herself a push and up in the air she went, followed by an equally hard fall.

She screamed loudly for her mother, who was preparing the evening meal.
That awful cry made her mother rush as fast as she could in the direction of the cry. Her mom was sad, but not surprised to see Brenda lying on the grass in pain. Her mom tried to raise her up, but Brenda could not stand.
She was taken to the Children's Hospital.
The doctors and nurses were very gentle with her.
They X-rayed her leg, found out that it was broken and applied a cast.
She had to spend a few days in the hospital.
While she was in the hospital she thought about school, her friends and how she had not listened to her mother.

Let's call all the words that are underlined in the story.

Brenda   brilliant   bright   branches   bruise breeze   broken

What sound do you hear at the beginning of each word?

The blend br

The 'br' sound is called a blend because you hear two different beginning sounds combining to make one sound. Let's make the sound again.

Look at the pictures and say the words.

brown

brick

bride

brownie

Say the words again and listen for the initial blend.

Use each word in a sentence and say each sentence aloud to your friends.

5.3 People who keep us safe

Workers who keep us safe

In every community, there are workers we depend on to keep us safe.
Here are some of them.

    police   firemen   soldiers   nurses   doctors

The police work with communities to make them better and safer.
The police protect us from dangers on the street.
They give tickets to motorists who break the rules on the road.
They protect our communities from criminals who want to rob and hurt people.

The firemen help to rescue people and animals from danger.
The firemen are always ready to put out the fires.
Their job is to save lives and property when there is a fire.
The firemen drive a fire truck with a long ladder.
They always wear helmets.

Soldiers defend our country from danger.
Sometimes they help the police carry out their duties.
When there are problems in some areas, the soldiers patrol with the police to keep law and order.

Doctors help to keep us strong and healthy. They use instruments like a stethoscope and a thermometer. Nurses work with doctors to keep us safe from diseases and other illnesses.
They immunise babies and young children at school too. The nurse at the clinic sees to it that we are fully immunised against diseases.

My doctor is a paediatrician.

Who is a paediatrician?

A paediatrician is a doctor who takes care of children.

Writing a business letter

Our school is observing Safety Week.
Our class wrote a letter inviting a safety officer to talk to the children.
Here is the letter the class wrote.

Mount Nebo Primary School
Benbow P.A.
St Catherine

November 23, 2006

The Safety Officer
Jamaica Fire Brigade
Linstead P.O.
St Catherine

Dear Sir,

Our school is celebrating Safety Week. We are inviting you to spend some time with us on Wednesday, to tell us about safety and to give us some safety tips.

I hope you will come and visit with us.

Yours truly,
Sean McKoy

How many addresses do you see in the letter?
There are two because this is a business letter.

When writing a business letter you must include the business address to the left below your address.

Measurement in kilometres and metres

The business letter on the left asks the fire safety officer to come from Linstead to the school at Benbow. How far does the officer have to travel?

The officer would have to drive a distance of about 20 kilometres. Long distances like this are usually measured in kilometres. Short distances are measured in metres.

Here is a map of a small town.

Page 141

Let us measure some distances on the map on page 141.
On this map a distance of 1 centimetre represents
100 metres in real life.

Look at the map.
The distance from the community centre to the
supermarket on the map is about 10 cm.
So in real life it is about 1000 metres.
The distance from the school to the police station on the
map is about 7 cm.
So in real life it is about 700 metres.

Let us measure the distance between two places on the
map using a piece of string.
Remember you are not a bird. You cannot go directly
from one place to another 'as the crow flies'. You have
to use the roads.

5.4 Taking medicine

Visiting the doctor

We should visit the doctor for regular check ups.

A person who is ill should visit the doctor.
The doctor prescribes medicine to help us get better.
Medicine is sometimes called *drugs*. It can be liquids or tablets.
It should be taken in the *dose* that the doctor says.
A dose can be a teaspoon or tablespoon of liquid or one or two tablets to be taken maybe one, two or three times every day.

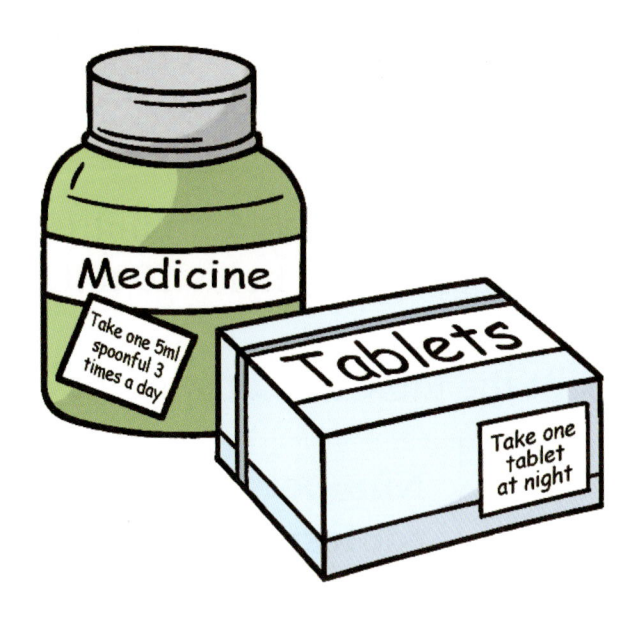

Sometimes people take too much medicine at one time.
We call this an *overdose*. This can be harmful.
When this happens the person can die.

Some people do not take drugs because they are ill.
They take them for fun.
People who take drugs for fun sometimes find they cannot stop doing it.
These people are called *drug addicts* or *drug abusers*.

Measuring medicine

We measure volumes in millilitres and litres.

When we visit the doctor and he prescribes medicine it is measured in millilitres (ml).
A millilitre is a small part of a litre.
There are 1000 millilitres in 1 litre.

A teaspoon (tsp) holds 5 millilitres.
A tablespoon (tblsp) holds 10 millilitres.

Look at the table and answer the questions below.

Number of teaspoons	Number of tablespoons	Number of millilitres
2	1	10 ml
4	2	20 ml
6	3	30 ml
8	4	40 ml

How many teaspoons hold the same as 1 tablespoon?
How many teaspoons hold 10 millilitres?
How many tablespoons hold 30 millilitres?

5.5 Helpful and harmful drugs

Helpful drugs

Some drugs protect us from diseases and help to make us well when we become ill.
These are called helpful drugs.

Doctors *prescribe* some of these helpful drugs. They cannot be bought over the counter without a prescription.

There are other helpful drugs that doctors do not need to prescribe for you. You can buy these drugs over the counter when you want to.

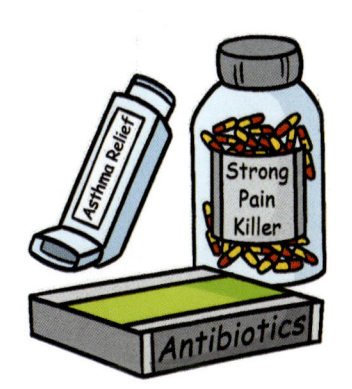

Some prescribed drugs are:

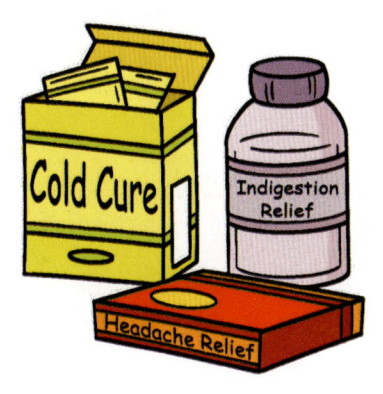

Some over-the-counter drugs are:

Harmful drugs

Some drugs may harm our bodies. These are called harmful drugs.
Harmful drugs may also be *illegal* drugs.
Some harmful drugs are known as crack, cocaine and ganja.

Illegal drugs can make people ill or even cause them to die.

Look at the picture. It shows some of the things that can happen to a person who takes illegal and harmful drugs.

addiction

illness

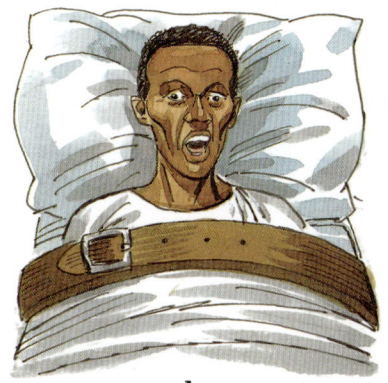

madness

death

You should always say NO to illegal and harmful drugs.

The blend dr

Listen to this sentence.

> The driver dropped the dry dress in a drum near Drake Drive.

What sound do you hear most often in the sentence?

The letters 'd' and 'r' combine together to make the 'dr' sound. It is called a blend.

Now let us read the sentence again together.

Look at the pictures and say the words.
They all begin with the sound 'dr'.

| dress | drum | drapes | drink | drugs | dray |

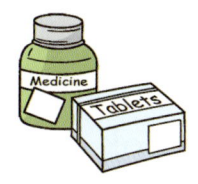

Turn to your friend and say the words stressing the 'dr' sound.

Comparing amounts of liquids

Containers hold different amount of liquid.

In small containers liquids are measured in millilitres.

Page 147

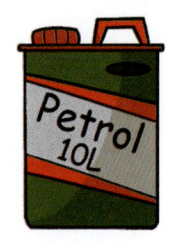

In large containers liquids are measured in litres.

Here is a litre container.

Name some liquids that are measured in millilitres and litres.

Look at the picture.

It will take 5 glasses of water to fill this litre bottle.
If I wanted to fill the litre bottle using the cup it would take 7 cups.

Your teacher will give you a litre container and some small containers.

Find two different sizes of small container.
Compare how many of each size it takes to fill the litre container.

5.6 Road signs

Road signs help motorists and pedestrians use the road safely.

Some road signs are for pedestrians while others are for motorists.

The stop sign tells motorists that they are to stop and give way to pedestrians and other motorists.

The railroad crossing sign tells us that train tracks run across the road. Motor vehicles should not stop on the tracks.

The school sign tells everyone that a school is nearby. Motorists should drive slowly when they see this sign.

A bus stop sign tells us where to take the bus.

Curved arrows tell us that the road is winding or that it has a bend.

The cross tell us that there is a crossroads ahead.

Shapes of road signs

Road signs have different shapes
Some are round and some are square.
Others look like curves and some are even shaped like the letter X.
The stop sign has eight sides.
It is called an *octagon*.

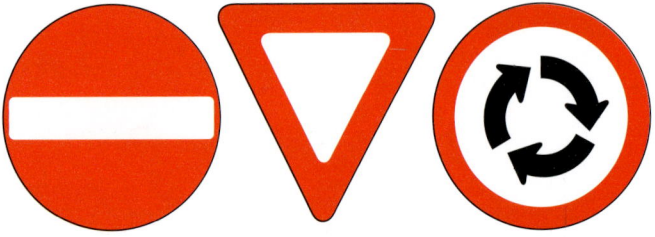

Look around your classroom and the school and say where you see signs giving warnings or information.

Page 150

5.7 Road safety

Accidents do happen

Many accidents happen on the roads. Sometimes people are injured in road accidents.

It is possible to get an *injury* even though we try very hard to avoid one.
An injury is damage to your body.

Sometimes you fall and bruise your skin, or even cut through your flesh.
You may injure or fracture a bone. When this happens a doctor is needed to fix it.
A doctor who fixes broken bones is called an *orthopaedic surgeon*.
Depending on where the broken bone is, you may need to wear a cast to hold the bone together until it gets better.

Next time the school nurse visits, or when you go to see the doctor, be sure to ask some questions about injuries and how they can be taken care of.

Write your questions and answers in your journals.

Accidents on the road and how they can be prevented

Have you ever been involved in an accident on the road? If so then talk to your friends about it.

Accidents can be prevented. Most road accidents are caused by speeding.
If motorists and pedestrians obeyed the rules of the road there would be fewer accidents.

Here are some causes of accidents and how they can be prevented.

Causes		How they can be prevented
Crossing the street in heavy traffic instead of following the directions of the traffic wardens or using the pedestrian crossing.		Use pedestrian crossings and obey the traffic warden.
Motorists disobeying traffic signals and signs may cause accidents with other vehicles as well as pedestrians.		Stop when the traffic light is on red.
Cyclists holding on to other vehicles while they are in motion. They are doing it for fun.		Ride your bicycle on the cycle paths and away from traffic.

Page 153

Motorists speeding along the road.

Drive within the given speed limit.

Playing in the streets and hopping moving vehicles. These dangerous habits often cause death.

Use the play field for all your games.

Safety rules

If we follow safety rules, accidents on the road can be prevented.

Here are some safety rules that you can follow:

NEVER …
- ✗ play in the streets.
- ✗ hop on to vehicles.
- ✗ play in the bus.
- ✗ wave your hands and head outside moving vehicles.

ALWAYS … ✓ use the footpath if there is one.
✓ ride your bicycle near to the sidewalk.
✓ walk on the right hand side of the road.
✓ look left and right before you cross the road.
✓ fasten your seatbelt.

Do you think these rules are sensible? Talk about them with your teacher.

Speed limit

Look at this road sign.

Read the sign. Have you ever seen one like this? What is it telling motorists?

Motorists are not to go faster than 50 kilometres per hour.

Good. This is called a *speed limit*.
You may be ticketed by the police if you travel faster than the speed limit that is set.

There are different speed limits for different roads and for different vehicles.

Vehicle	Limit on highways	Limit in areas with houses
car	80 kilometres per hour	50 kilometres per hour
truck	50 kilometres per hour	30 kilometres per hour

5.8 Accidents at school

Safety at school

Let us read this poem together.

Poem:

We all say, SAFETY FIRST!
We do not shove
We do not push
We walk in lines when we must
We wait our turn.

We clean up spills
So no one slides and falls
Sharp objects we only use
When we are supervised
If an accident should happen
We'd call our teacher right away.

Discuss this poem with the person next to you.

Look at the pictures on the next page. They show some of the things that cause accidents at school.

✗ These rails should be used as support when walking up or down the stairs.

✗ When children run or play along corridors, they can be involved in accidents that may cause injuries to themselves and others.

✗ Materials and equipment should be properly stored. Equipment used for experiments, projects and art should be put away when not in use.

✗ Brooms and other things that will cause people to trip and fall should be securely stored.

✗ When the classroom is used as a playing field children can trip and fall over the furniture.

Page 157

Where can accidents happen at school?

Many accidents happen at school.
As at home and on the road, there are many unsafe areas on the school compound.

Here is a picture of a school compound.
The unsafe areas are marked for you in red.

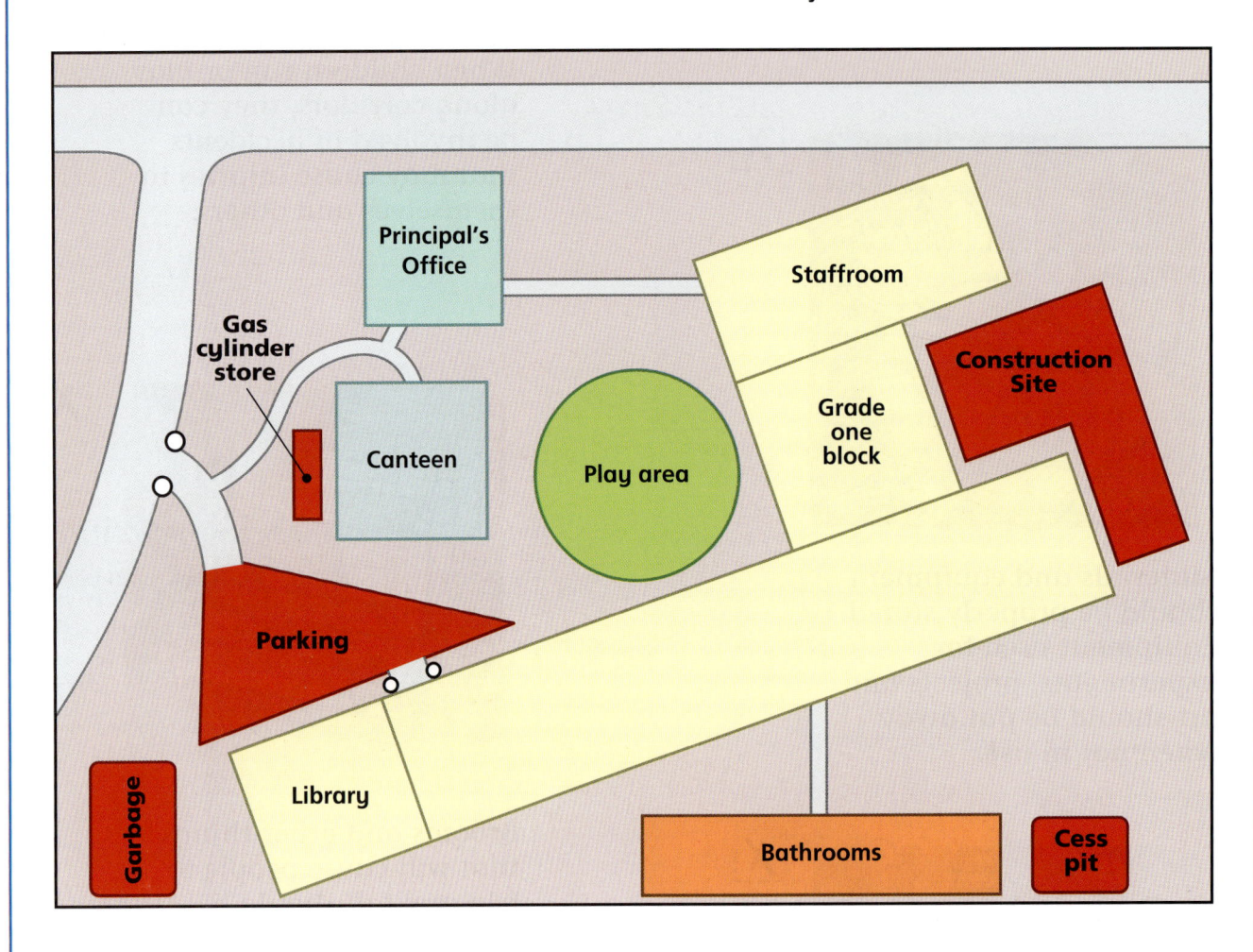

Name some safe and unsafe areas at your school.

Showing information on a pictograph

Sometimes students do go to unsafe areas at school and accidents happen.

Look at this pictograph. It shows the different kinds of injuries that students suffered at my school *this* year.

Type of injury	Number of students this year
cut	👦👦👦👦👦
bruise	👦👦👦👦👦👦👦
broken bone	👦👦
sprain	👦👦👦👦

Look at this other pictograph. It shows the different kinds of injuries that students suffered at my school *last* year.

Type of injury	Number of students last year
cut	👦👦👦👦👦👦
bruise	👦👦👦👦👦👦👦👦
broken bone	👦👦👦👦👦
sprain	👦👦👦👦👦👦

Let us talk about the injuries.
Has my school become a safer place since last year?
Why do you think so?

5.9 Making school a safe place

Safety rules for school

Schools have rules.
To be safe at school, everyone must obey these rules.
You should also encourage others to do the same.

Here are some of the rules. You may know a few of them already.

Don't …
- ✗ play on the furniture.
- ✗ stand on the hand rails.
- ✗ climb over fences.
- ✗ run down the stairs.

Think of some more things you shouldn't do.

Do …
- ✓ put garbage in the bins.
- ✓ put books and equipment away at the end of lessons.
- ✓ put away brooms and mops.
- ✓ walk quietly down corridors.

Think of some more things you should do.

Safety drills at school

Safety drills help to prepare us for what to do if there is an earthquake or a fire at school.
They should be practised by everyone.

Earthquake

Students should learn to do the right thing if there is an earthquake.

If there is an earthquake, students should hide under a desk or table and stay there until it is safe to come out.

Fire

Students should learn to do the right thing if there is a fire.

If there is a fire, students should crawl below the heavy smoke to safety. Never panic, especially if there are stairs to go down.

How often are earthquake and fire drills done at your school?

5.10 First aid

We are members of our school's Red Cross Club.

We give first aid to people who have had accidents. The accidents that we treat include cuts, burns, nail scratches, broken bones and insect bites.

We take instructions from our teacher who is trained in giving first aid.
We have a big first aid kit at school.
Here is what is in our first aid kit.

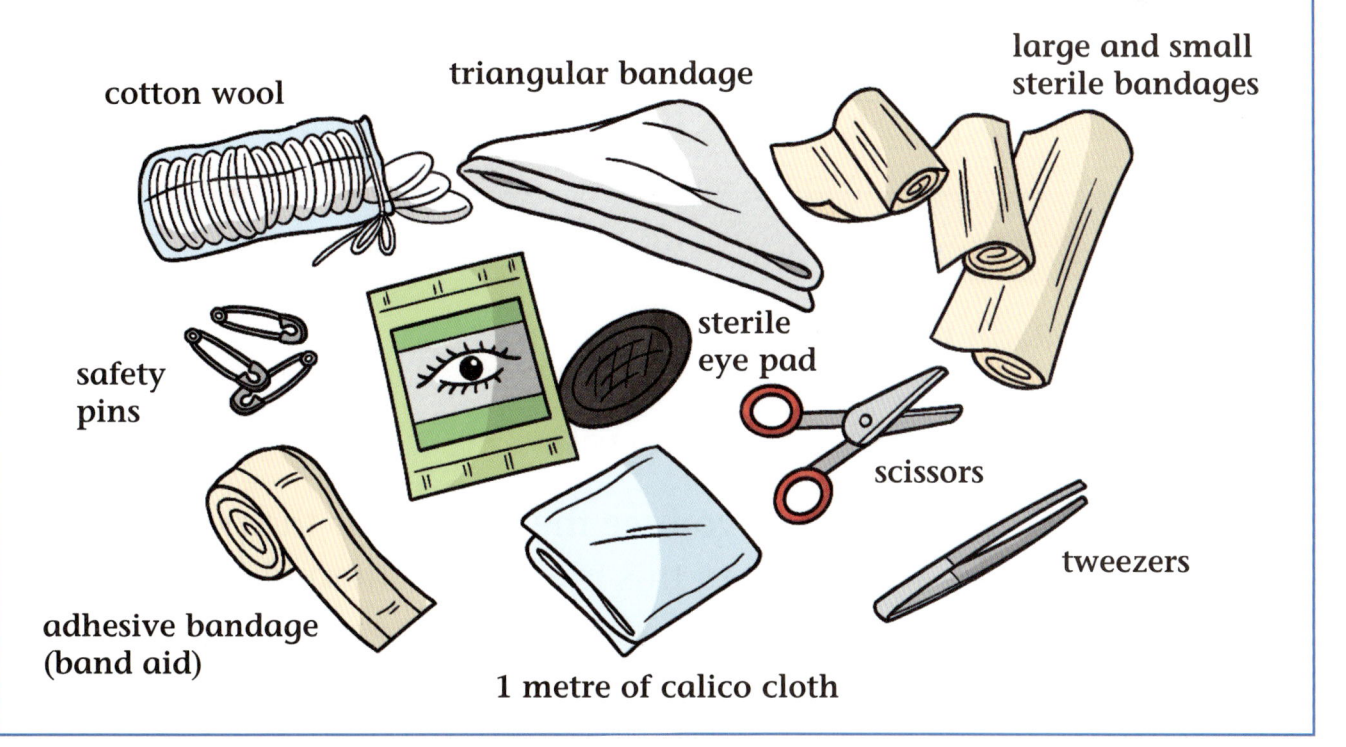

cotton wool

triangular bandage

large and small sterile bandages

safety pins

sterile eye pad

scissors

tweezers

adhesive bandage (band aid)

1 metre of calico cloth

Pictograph of adhesive dressings

This pictograph shows the number and sizes of adhesive dressings that are in the class first aid kit.

Dressing	Number in first aid kit
small round	○ ○ ○
large round	○ ○
oval	○ ○ ○ ○ ○
square	☐ ☐ ☐ ☐ ☐ ☐ ☐
rectangular	▭ ▭ ▭ ▭ ▭ ▭ ▭

Answer these questions about the different kinds of adhesive dressings.

How many adhesive dressings are in the kit?
How many are egg-shaped (oval)?
How many are round?

More about listening and safety

Read this story.

Story: **If Only I'd Listened**

'Hey Jack! Did you see the fence near the pond when you were coming this morning?' shouted Bill from across the room.
'No, I did not see it, what happened to it?' replied Jack.

'The barbed wire is broken, so we can swing on it, or even use it as a short cut to go fishing in the pond,' said Bill.

Just then the teacher came into the room.
'Now children,' she said, 'there was an accident over the weekend and the fence at the back of the school was broken. Please do not go near the area as it is not safe.'
Jack and Bill smiled to themselves, because they already had a plan.
At the sound of the break bell they rushed towards the fence.
They were so happy to see the open area, they did not look where they were going.
'Lord have mercy, I can't move!' cried Jack.
'What happened?' called Bill.
As Jack turned, Bill saw a long rip in his trousers and a bright red spot.

The wire had cut through the pants and into Jack's flesh. He was bleeding.

Someone ran to get Mr Smith from the Red Cross Link.
Mr Smith lifted Jack off the wire, and took him to the sick bay.
After the wound was cleaned and bandaged, Jack was taken to the hospital where he received several stitches.
At the hospital Jack kept saying, 'If only I'd listened, I would not be hurt like this.'

Discuss the story with the person next to you.

6 How do others take care of me?

6.1 Adults care for me

Adults take care of me

Read this conversation between the Grade two students and their teacher.

Teacher: Boys and girls, today we will talk about the adults in your homes who take care of you. Michael, who takes care of you?

Michael: My mother and father, and grandmother, always take good care of me.

Joan: I live with my uncle and aunt. They love me a lot.

Teacher: Boys and girls, what about the adults outside the home?

Suzzette: Miss, I like to spend time with my godparents. They help me with my homework.

John: My teachers help me to read and write. I love them.

May: My parents always take me to see the doctor or nurse, and the dentist. They see to it that I am healthy.

Oliver: I want to be a soldier, a police officer or a security guard. I want to help people to be safe.

Teacher: Well, boys and girls, all these people should be your friends. They help to take care of you.

Ask your parents about other people in the community who show that they care for you.

Parents and family members

My parents and family have a special responsibility to care for me.
They started caring for me from the day I was born.
They love me.

They provide me with food, clothing and shelter. Sometimes they take me to see the doctor or nurse, or the dentist. They want to make sure I am healthy.

A doctor who takes care of young children is called a pediatrician.

My parents teach me how to keep safe. They keep harmful objects out of the way. They do not want anything to harm me.

What harmful objects do your parents keep out of your way?

Say these important words.

    care   **dentist**   **paediatrician**   **responsible**
    shelter   **vaccine**

Discuss the meanings of these words with your friend.

Adding -ing to verbs

Some verbs are words that show action.

Read these action words:

    swim   run   mop   sit   chop

When we talk about something that a person or thing is doing we sometimes add 'ing' to the root word.
There are some words that need help before the 'ing' can be added.

Look at the pictures and read the sentences.

He is swimming.    Pauline is running.    Father is mopping the floor.    The cat is sitting on the mat.    Uncle Peter is chopping wood.

Notice that the last letter was doubled before 'ing' was added.

Think of some other action words that must have their last letter doubled before 'ing' is added. Use three of the words you thought of to make sentences.

Making money calculations

Polly made a bet with Tim that she had saved more money in her saving pan. When they checked the money in their saving pans, Polly found that she had two 50 dollar notes. Tim counted two 20 dollar coins and one 10 dollar coin. Polly won her bet. She had saved 100 dollars while Tim had saved only 50 dollars.

Page 171

Here are some pictures of some of our Jamaican money.

Here are some different ways that money can be divided.

Amount	Can be divided into
$100	$50 + $50
$50	$20 + $20 + $10
$20	$10 + $10
$10	$5 + $5
$5	$1 + $1 + $1 + $1 + $1

Talk to your friends about other ways in which these amounts of money can be divided.

Adults also cared for Jesus

Read this story about Jesus when He was young.

Story: **Jesus is Found in the Temple**

Mary and Joseph loved their son Jesus very much. They hid him from Herod who wanted to kill Him when he was a baby. They always took Jesus with them wherever they went. One day Mary and Joseph could not find Jesus. They were very worried. They asked some friends to help them to find their son.

Mary and Joseph found Jesus in the Temple. He was talking to some men and women.

Read the story again and talk to your friends about how Mary and Joseph showed that they cared for Jesus.

You can also read this story in the Bible in Luke 2: 41-50.

6.2 Growing up

As I grow up I still need the care and protection of adults.

Read the jingle. Note all of the things that you can now do.

Jingle:

I brush my teeth
I lace my shoes
I feed myself
I comb my hair
I am grown up you see!

Look what I do.
I skip, I dance,
I hop, I jump
I even do a twist, you see
I'm older now
I can do things
That as a babe I couldn't do.

I still need granny, mom and dad
My teacher, nurse, the policeman too
They love me so
They care for me in every way.

Read the jingle again. This time do all the actions while you read.

Playing with words

Read each pair of sentences below.
The words that are underlined sound alike, but have different spellings and meanings.

| waist | Tammie has a belt around her <u>waist</u>. |
| waste | Do not <u>waste</u> the water Joudy-Ann. |

| too | Are you coming <u>too</u>? |
| two | I have <u>two</u> pens in my bag. |

so	<u>So</u>, where have you been?
sew	Mother loves to <u>sew</u> my dresses.
sow	I am going to <u>sow</u> the seeds.

Talk to your teacher about the meanings of these words.
Add them to your class dictionary.

6.3 Health care

Nurses and doctors help to keep us healthy.
They teach us good hygiene and healthy living.

I practise good hygiene when I wash my hands.

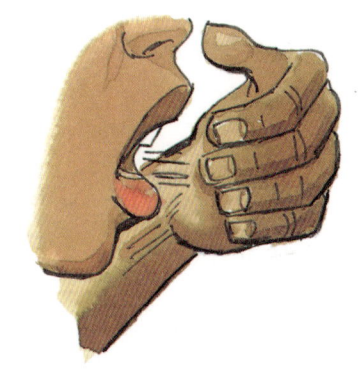

I should cover my mouth when I am coughing.

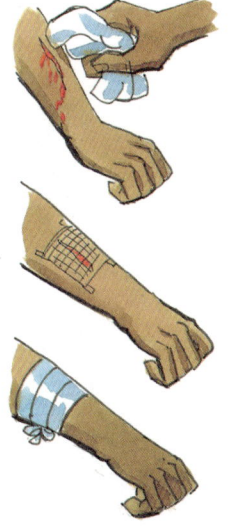

If I get a cut or a graze I should clean it, dress it and cover it. I don't want to get germs into it.

6.4 People who care

There are children who do not have parents to care for them. Other people in the community care for them. Some of these children join new families and live with them in their homes. Other children live with caring adults in special homes called *orphanages*.

Some children are disabled.
Specially trained people are sometimes needed to help look after them.

Some children in the Bible were cared for by adults who were not their parents.
Eli the priest cared for Samuel.
Moses grew up in the palace with his sister and the princess cared for him.

Samuel and Moses became great men. They loved and cared for people.

6.5 Let us show we care

There are many ways to show someone you care. You may hug or kiss them. You may say kind words to them.

We should say thanks to our parents, friends, teachers and other persons who care for us.

We should always show others that we care.

Tell your friends what you do to show that you care for others.

Caring for the environment

Read this passage.

We live in a beautiful world and we should take care of it.

We should not dump garbage in gullies and rivers, and on beaches.
Instead we should place our garbage in covered bins and drums.
We should keep our rivers and beaches clean.

We should keep our school yards, parks and other public places clean.

Trees are beautiful.
Tree roots hold the soil together. They help to prevent the ground from drying out.
They provide shade for people and animals.
They make the air clean and fresh.
We should not destroy our trees.

God cares

God cares for us.
He provides many sources of food.
He gives us trees, plants and flowers.
He provides birds, animals, seas, rivers and other people to make the world a happy place.

God cares about his children and wants them to be happy. He sent his son to live on Earth to help people.

> For God so loved the world, that he gave his only begotten son, that whosoever believeth in him should not perish, but have eternal life.
>
> *St John 3:16*

More about caring for animals

Read this story.

Story: **Caring for Milly**

Milly is my pet dog.
She is very frisky and I love her very much.

I got Milly when she was still a puppy.
She is brown and white.
I feed her well and I brush her.
I exercise with her every day. I take her to the veterinarian to make sure that she is healthy.
Milly had five puppies today.
Daddy thinks I should give them as gifts to some of my friends.

I will be sad to see them go, but I think that daddy is right.

A friendly letter (revision)

Fair Prospect Primary School
Fair Prospect P.O.
January 6, 2006

Dear Gordon,

Milly had five puppies this morning. I will be giving them as gifts to my friends. Daddy says that it will be hard to care for five puppies. I would like to give you one. Please let me know if you want him. Please give him a lovely name.

Your friend,

Ethan

Read the letter Gordon wrote to his friend Ethan. The sentences all begin with a capital letter and end with a full stop.

All your telling sentences should begin with a capital letter and end with a full stop.

How many sentences are in this letter? I hope you found six sentences.
Read each sentence aloud to your friend.

Verbs (revision)

Some verbs are called action words. If Gordon is to take good care of Milly's puppy he will have to feed, bath and exercise him. He will also need to brush his fur and wash his feeding trays regularly. Feed, bath, exercise, brush and wash are all verbs. These verbs are action words.

Think of other action words and share them with your friends.

Problem solving

Here are some problems in mathematics.
Let us read them together and then solve them.

Problem 1

Milly had five puppies. I gave two puppies to friends. How many are left?

To find the answer to the problem we take 2 puppies away from 5 puppies.
We can show it in this way:

$$5 - 2 = 3$$ So I have 3 puppies left.

Problem 2

I am eight years old and I can now brush my teeth all by myself. Five years ago I couldn't do this. How old was I five years ago?

To solve this problem we take 5 years away from 8 years.

We can show it in this way:

$$8 - 5 = 3$$ So I was 3 years old.

Tammie's chart

Here is a chart showing how different family members help Tammie.

Mother and Father	Grandmother Lindo	Aunt Hope	Uncle Phillip
Take her to school	Packs lunch	Combs her hair	Takes her to school
Pick her up	Reads her stories	Cooks meals	Picks her up
Dress her	Takes her to the park		
Shop and cook for her			

Here we see that five family members help Tammie. Her parents and uncle take her to and from school.

Talk about how other family members care for Tammie.